A Pimp's Life

A Pimp's Life

Treasure Hernandez

www.urbanbooks.net

Urban Books, LLC
78 East Industry Court
Deer Park, NY 11729

A Pimp's Life © Copyright 2009 Urban Books, LLC

ISBN 13: 978-1-60162-529-8
ISBN 10: 1-60162-529-4

First Mass Market Printing November 2012
First Trade Printing February 2009
Printed in the United States of America

10 9 8 7 6 5 4 3 2 1

This is a work of fiction. Any references or similarities to actual events, real people, living or dead, or to real locales are intended to give the novel a sense of reality. Any similarity in other names, characters, places, and incidents is entirely coincidental.

Distributed by Kensington Publishing Corp.
Submit Wholesale Orders to:
Kensington Publishing Corp.
C/O Penguin Group (USA) Inc.
Attention: Order Processing
405 Murray Hill Parkway
East Rutherford, NJ 07073-2316
Phone: 1-800-526-0275
Fax: 1-800-227-9604

Prologue

My moms died today. The monster finally devoured her spirit and life. She lived HIV-positive for fifteen years before finally succumbing to full-blown AIDS. She was sick the whole time through before that anyway.

Drugs fucked up her whole shit years ago. Fucked my whole shit up too. I watched her get high every day. It used to make me cry to see her after she hit that pipe. She'd be so lost in space. It was like her soul wasn't there. But her body was always there for anyone who could keep her the highest. I guess she finally reached that mountaintop she'd been climbing to for so long.

What sense did it make though, when all she did was fall off? Maybe my father could've given her a helping hand—if she knew who that was. She had a child with a man from Virginia three years before I was born. She never knew what it was, and she didn't want to know. She put it up for adoption the instant the baby was born.

I may as well have been adopted too because I didn't like the idea of admitting that my moms was a crackhead ho. She didn't love me. All she ever loved was that pipe. You know how that shit makes me feel? It don't make me feel like nothing because if you ain't never known love, then you ain't going to miss love.

Chapter One

Mack

I shielded my eyes from the glare of the afternoon sun as I walked out of Queens Courthouse. It had been a long night. I'd just spent it serving nine hours behind bars, thanks to the brave and dedicated hard work of New York City's Finest. I walked down the long row of cement steps and stood at the curb. The traffic lights were out, and cars headed east and west whizzed by with no regard for pedestrians trying to make a dash for the island that divided the flow of traffic. I stood under the DON'T WALK sign and pressed the button to no avail.

"Fuck it," I said, running into the street as soon as I saw an opening. I jumped on top of the divider and looked to my immediate right. Cars raced up the street as if this were the "Ghetto 500." My heart pounded through my chest from running, and my adrenaline rushed like Russell's when he

was up in that elevator catching the full force of a
J.B. beat-down.

Soon as I hit the sidewalk my cell rang. "Yo," I
said, panting heavily, gasping for air.

"You get out yet, jailbird?" Sade laughed.

Sade was my woman. We lived together in a
house in Queens Village. She wasn't the best-
looking woman I'd dealt with, but she had a good
heart. Sade was five foot six inches and was dark-
skinned, with full lips like Fantasia. Originally
from Virginia, she'd moved to New York three
years ago after her stepfather, Glen, raped her.
When she brought the issue to her mom's attention, her mom flipped the script by accusing her
of lying and trying to cause a rift in her stable
relationship.

When Sade's moms finally did confront Glen
with the charges, he denied it, swearing up and
down every crack of ass he'd ever licked that Sade
came on to him. Deep in her heart, she knew she
was wrong, so she let her daughter go and moved
right along. She knew Sade was telling the truth
and that he'd always had his eye on her. I mean,
why not? Here you had this young woman physi-
cally blossoming right before your eyes versus a
sickly, one-titty lady, slowly but surely withering
away.

Afraid of spending the last years of her life home alone, she chose his side, with her head down to the floor. That still bothered Sade to this day. She didn't understand how you could love somebody your entire life then just turn your back on them. None of the men her mother dated had good intentions.

Sade's moms was dying of breast cancer and had a huge life insurance policy. Every eligible bachelor in Richmond knew that she was worth four hundred thousand dollars after her ass expired. All she wanted was to not die alone.

Sade would call her every now and again, but Glen always answered the phone and hung up when he heard her voice. Eventually he had the number changed, and Sade lost contact with her and refused to go visit her long as he was still living there.

"Yeah. I'm free. About to grab me some New York Fried Chicken from the Habeebs." I walked inside the restaurant. "Call Anton and tell him I said to come and get me. It's his fault I was in there in the first place," I said, sitting down. "Yo, Ahmed, let me get two thighs, small fries, and a lemon Mystic Iced Tea, man," I said to the owner. "Yeah, so, baby, did you miss me?"

"You know I did."

"Uh-huh. You better had."

"Whatever, Mack. I'm about to see the Dominicans. My hair needs to be washed and wrapped."

"Don't be out there spending up a whole lot of money, Sade. You heard?"

"Love you," she said, disconnecting the call.

I walked inside my Queens Village home and flopped down on the blue leather couch. I had been up the entire night madder than a muthafucka, sitting up in jail on some bullshit marijuana charge. I don't even smoke. My dude Anton was blowing one of them thangs down while we was inside Cambria Heights Park with these two bitches. I don't know which was faster, the detectives who rolled up in the park in the black Expedition with tinted windows, or Anton's warrant-having ass hopping over the five-foot gate at the end of the park. He dropped the cigar shit right in front of me. So guess who it belonged to, according to the law? They let the girls off with a warning and let me ride in back of the truck with them.

The doorbell rang just as I'd reached my comfort zone level. I ignored it at first, but the person continued to pound the fucking bell out. I looked through the peephole. "Ay, yo, who the fuck is it?"

Anton's big-ass head was all up in my view. I'm looking out the hole, his silly, non-complex ass is trying to look in.

"Open the door, man. You know I got warrants." He looked around before quickly rushing inside. Then he held out his hand. "Hey, man, apologies for last night."

"You's an ill dude, yo. I ain't fucking with you no more outside. I don't like being locked up. You just bounced without saying a word."

"If there was time to say anything, I would of. Look, I can't afford to get caught by these pigs, yo. They'll kill me. That's what they do when you shoot one of theirs."

I walked to the refrigerator, pulled two Heinekens from the top shelf, and popped the caps. "Whatever, man. Did you ever speak to them girls in Brooklyn . . . Kim's people?"

"Aw, man, I was caught up in some next shit, son. But I'ma get up with her tonight and shit. Matter of fact, you should come too. She keep asking about you."

"Naw. I'm chilling at home with Sade. I didn't get to give her no daddy good loving last night because of your ass." I pointed at him.

Anton took a long swig of the beer. "Gordy was asking about you too."

"Yeah? I don't hear my phone ringing off the hook. He ain't looking for me. He looking for something about me."

"Well, whatever the fuck"—he held out his hand—"I'm about to be out. Just came to check in on you and make sure you wasn't violated in the shower." Anton laughed.

"Fuck you!" I laughed. "Get the hell out my house," I said, pushing him out and closing the door.

Chapter Two

Mack

"I'm thinking about taking a trip to see my mother." Sade sat up in the bed. She leaned her back against the headboard and touched my chest. "You heard me, baby?"

"Naw. What's up?" I said, my eyes still closed.

"I said I want to see my mother. What do you think about that?"

"Sade," I said, sitting up, "if you want to see your mother, I'll roll with you down there. It's nothing."

"No, I need to do this by myself. I'll be all right."

"What about ol' boy?"

"I'll worry about that when I get there."

"You sure?"

"I'm a big girl, baby. I'll be cool."

"A'ight. I know you can handle yourself. So when you leaving?"

"I'm driving down there next Friday. I'll be gone for about three days."

I kissed her cheek.

"What was that for?"

"For being a real thorough bitch. That's the shit right there that made me fall in love with you."

Sade reached her hand under the covers and placed it on my hardening dick, massaging the head with her thumb. "And that's the shit that made me fall in love with you," she said, removing the covers from over me. She pulled my boxers off and slowly slid her mouth around the head of my dick and sucked it like a swollen thumb, licking around the rim and poking at the eye with the tip of her tongue.

I lay on my back looking at her, as she widened her mouth and long-throated the nine inches of "bless you with my loving." She gagged once, she gagged twice, but maintained the sexual discipline required to control tossing it up. When my body shivered, she sucked even harder.

"Awwww Shiiiit," I yelled out. "Sade. Oh my damn," I cried out as she continued milking the cow.

"What's the matter, boo? You can't take it?" she asked, my love fluids leaking from the corners of her mouth. "Where the freak at, daddy?"

She rolled her tongue around at me then stuck it down my throat.

I lifted off her shirt and sucked on her hard, erect nipples, my mouth cruising around, on, and between her firm titties. I licked from her neck down to her navel and spoke to it in tongues. I melted down in between her legs and sniffed my pussy. And craved my pussy. I watched it as it throbbed and leaked in anticipation of a forthcoming tsunami.

"Come on, daddy, I wanna see lakes running down these sheets," she said, rubbing them with one hand while the other was snug behind my head.

I made her butterfly wings flap and her cat sing for Tender Vittles. I eloquently ran my tongue around the edges of each wing then quickly slid it further down. I pushed it up into her ass, and she sighed loudly. I razzled her and dazzled her with *tongue*nastic flips and twists, and turns and churns.

And then she farted in my fucking face. I was done.

"What happened, daddy?" Sade rubbed between her legs.

"Come on, man, how many times you going to fart in my face?"

She laughed. "Did it stink?"

"Oh, you think that shit is funny now, huh?" I playfully grabbed her by the shoulders and lay back down. "Come on, ma, get on top." I was standing strong as ever.

Sade sat on it, and it slid straight up inside of her, the soft walls collapsing around me then constricting. As I lay still for a moment and let it burn, my body ushered in an even harder erection.

She planted her palms on my chest and slowly began to gyrate her hips a li'l something. She heard my blacksnake moan and matched it with a pleasurable meow. She leaned forward and grabbed my shoulders then began popping that thing up and down like a piston.

As we stared and growled at each other with the ferocity of a tiger and tigress, I grabbed her around the hips to secure her in place.

Sade threw her free hand in the air and slapped her own ass then froze, dragging her nails across my chest. "Baby, I'm about to cum." She grabbed my wrists. "Baby, I'm about to c-c-cum," she said, bracing herself this time. "Here it cuummss," she yelled, happily rolling off me then laying absolutely still.

"Now that shit right there, baby"—I kissed her lips—"that shit right there was the best sex we ever had."

"Y—y—yeah," she responded, still a little shaken. "Maybe you need to spend the night in jail a little more often," she joked.

"That ain't funny," I said in all seriousness.

"Oh, you just need to stop it, Mack." Sade kissed my deflating showstopper. "Oh, what's going on here?" She lifted up ol' flappy. "Why you look so down?" She smiled at it. "You want mommy to make you happy again?"

I shook its head yes, and she went on ahead and made that fallen soldier a master sergeant.

Chapter Three

Mack

I was filling my gas-guzzling black Suburban up with some super unleaded at a Gulf gas station in Elmont, Long Island. Anton was in my passenger seat, smoking a Philly and bopping his head to one of R. Kelly's cheaters-only anthems.

"I should take this shit to the carwash." I ran my finger across the door. "Every time it rains, I gotta get this shit washed." A horn beeped from behind my truck. I paid no attention to it, until it beeped again.

Anton looked out his window toward the back of the truck. "Be easy," he yelled out. "We almost done."

The horn beeped again, and I walked over to the green Infiniti, ready to knock somebody out. Pineapple-scented fresheners inside the car released a fragrance that clawed at the air when the window rolled down.

It had Virginia license plates and a decent-sounding stereo. The woman behind the wood grain looked so good, I almost forgot why I walked over there in the first place.

She was brown-skinned with chinky eyes and high cheekbones. Her lips were thin and coated with earth-toned gloss. She wore her hair cut short but straight, a couple of spikes toward the side of her head.

She turned her music down. "Well, what you want, playa?"

"Why you keep beeping that horn behind us? You see how big that truck is? It takes a minute to fill up, you know."

"I got an appointment to get to. Traffic is going to be straight bananas on the Cross Island." She looked over at the traffic under the crosswalk.

"You'll make it. My shit should just about be filled."

I walked to the pump and pulled the hose out my gas tank. "You could've said the shit was finished," I said, looking at Anton as I activated the auto-start. I pulled over some then walked back to her after she got out to pump her gas. "Hey, I'm sorry about that earlier." I extended my hand. "I thought you was some dick trying to be a smart ass. My name's Mack."

"No, it was just li'l ol' me." She smiled and bent over to pick up the gas card she'd dropped.

Looking at her in the car, it was hard to tell that her legs were so thick, but she was firm and muscular, like really stacking. "So what's your name, love?" I looked down at my watch. I'd almost forgotten that we had somewhere to be too.

"Joi," she said, keeping an eye on the price of the gas tank. She placed the nozzle back in the holder and stood in front of me, her arms folded.

"Anyway, I do promotions at Club Phenomenon, down Rockaway Boulevard. I thought maybe one day you and some of your girlfriends could come through and show some love. We could always use a new face up in there, a fresh, fine face such as yours. First few drinks on me."

She looked at me and laughed. She put the hand down on the hood of her car to support herself from falling over. "You is mad corny, yo. Is that your best line?"

"Naw. My best lines come in li'l baggies about this size." I demonstrated with my fingers.

"Yeah? Well, I'm good on that. What you tryin'a holla for anyway? You all cute in the face and whatnot, I know you got wifey at home biting her nails down to the cuticle."

"Not even. I won't front though. I do have a lot of friends."

"Friends, huh? So I guess you just want me to be one of your new friends? Homie, lover, friend, fuck buddy?"

"Yo, that's not even how I'm coming at you. Them other niggaz got your mind wrong. I just saw a pretty lady and took a chance. Besides, you never know when you may need a friend like me."

"Oh really? Let me ask you something? Do it look like I might be needing a friend's help anytime soon?" Joi chuckled. "Oh, you thought because I'm from VA your New York accent was going to give you some sort of leeway into some drawers? I don't have time for this. I'm out." She opened her car door.

I totally ignored the bullshit Joi was spitting. "You got a man, Joi?"

"Something like that."

"A'ight. So let's cut the small talk. Here goes a flyer and my card. Come on down and have a good time, baby. Promise, you won't regret it." I smiled.

Joi looked at me over her shades for a second then reached down into the cup holder inside her car. She handed me her number. "You can call me after seven P.M. during the week. That's when my minutes start." She laughed.

"I hear ya, baby. So that's what's up. I'ma holla at you real soon."

She stepped inside her car, beeping as she pulled off toward the Cross Island Parkway. Getting inside the truck, I said to Anton, "Now that's how you recruit, boy."

"Anybody could've done that. All you did was give the bitch a flyer. So what that mean? You keep talking about this pimping shit, but I ain't seen shit yet. You be fucking the strippers for free and all, but you not pimping."

"You'll see. Look at me, I am a gorgeous muthafucka, and women love that. Don't ever let no bitch tell you that looks don't matter. This is where it's at." I stroked my goatee. "This fly shit right here." I smiled, looking in my rearview, and pushed back my bushy eyebrows. "Personality is for psychologists," I said as I headed down Linden Boulevard.

A white-and-blue Q4 bus stopped at a red light in front of us and released a cloud of smog. "Close the windows," I said, turning on the vent. "This is why I hate coming down this block. I'm taking the back street." I turned left on 227th.

"So what you and Cocaine was talking about?"

"I'll let you know. Don't be opening your mouth about it either when we get to his house. You know how that nigga be getting when dudes start asking about shit he didn't bring up to them himself."

"I ain't worried about his ass. He might've put OPT together, but I'm the cat that be putting in all the work."

Cocaine, founder of OPT, On Point Killers, had more schemes, scams, and smarts than any man I ever knew. OPT was a team of thorough wolves based solely in New York City, known for getting that paper, and stomping in a head or two, if it came down to it. Non-believers became victims of the human pool table effect, eight balls in the corner pockets of our younger shorties-in-training hugging the block as if it were a surrogate father.

Cocaine was forty-six and straight out of an old school called "hard-knock life." He was sentenced to ten years in prison when he was sixteen for killing Watty, his mother's boyfriend. Watty was beating the shit out of his mother one night and knocked her through a glass coffee table. Cocaine shot him with a gun he was holding for a friend. According to Cocaine, his mother only respected Watty when he was applying that chokehold around her scrawny little neck. And she only seemed to follow orders when she got a slap across the lips.

Even though it was some fucked-up shit to grow up seeing, it opened son's eyes in understanding a bitch. They wanted a man to be in control, to tell them what to do, and even welcomed a beating, minor or major, if they consciously ever stepped out of line.

All throughout Cocaine's entire life, he ain't never saw any man love his mother. She never asked for respect. She was a poor excuse and a walking embarrassment in his eyes because, after it was really all said and done, it turned out his moms was a prostitute and a dope fiend. It was still etched in his head, the day he came home from school and his moms was fucking and doing dope right on his bed. Now if his own momma wasn't shit and he never felt what it was like to know that kind of love, how in the fuck could anybody ever expect that man to love and respect another woman?

Me and Cocaine met when I did two years of fed time for gun-running. We spent the last two years of his bid exchanging ideas. We got along so good that when I came home he had a spot for me in Queens Village and a li'l Honda Civic at the time. When I was put down with OPT, everything changed.

Cocaine had a stable of bitches working for him, regular bitches with jobs, others just trying to make a dollar. My job was to recruit for him. His clients consisted of average niggaz, white boys from Long Island and the Upper East Side of Manhattan, police, and some anonymous rappers. His biggest clientele was the husbands tired of the same ol' sloppy, aged, wrinkled pussy they was getting after twenty years of marriage and who left their desperate housewives crying their eyes out at home.

A lot of dudes was jealous because I didn't have to go through the initiation process they did. I got in because he knew I could make that dough for him. And if one more of them faggots questioned why I didn't get beat in, they'd be dead.

Cocaine usually didn't have to say anything twice. He had a short fuse. And an even shorter one when it came to his woman, Cakes, an ex-stripper from Michigan that he scooped at a party. She was on the books too. After he'd showed her what kind of bank he was dealing with, she was on the first Greyhound running. She was the epitome of what a dime should look like, five nine, slender, bronze complexion. Her name was tatted across her chest and was followed by "Cocaine's Property."

She was his main investment, but there was a problem. He beat on her so bad at times that she couldn't always look presentable enough to work. He didn't like no one in the family looking at her unless she was on duty. She was *his* woman.

"Yo!" I knocked on Cocaine's front door. I said to Anton as he got out my truck, "Leave that window cracked so that shit don't be like no oven when we leave." I rapped on the door again. "Yo!"

"Who it is? What it be like?" he said, answering the door in a robe. "Pimping." He smiled. "What's happening, broth?" He widened the door so we could enter.

"You know me. I just bc doing what it do," I responded, standing in the patio.

"What's up, Ton? You gonna come in, or you just gonna stand there like a fucking porch monkey?" Cocaine laughed. "Get your ass on in here." He looked up and down the street before closing the door. He said to Anton, "You get my new strippers for the club yet?"

"I'm still working on it. The girl ain't been home. What you want me to do?" Anton shrugged his shoulders.

"Yeah, you absolutely right. What the fuck he gonna do, Mack?" Cocaine shook his head as we walked into the living room. He walked over to the stereo. "Y'all niggaz want something to drink?"

"You got some Grey Goose?" Anton asked.

"Yeah." Cocaine searched for the remote to his stereo. "What you want, Pimping?"

Before I could answer, his phone rang.

"Yeah," he answered. "Look, Trish, you have your ass here before eight tonight. That's it," he said and disconnected the call.

No sooner had he stuck it down in the pocket of his robe than it rang again. He looked down at the caller ID display and frowned. "Looky here, y'all, I gotta take this call upstairs. Make your own drinks. You know where they at." He pressed power on the remote then jogged up the stairs.

The front door unlocked, and in walked Cakes, her hands filled with shopping bags. She was absolutely fucking gorgeous, man. She closed the door with the heel of her foot. "What's good, y'all?" She placed her bags in front of a blue re-clining lounge chair next to a four-foot potted bella palm tree, where an automatic sterling silver mini-sprinkler connected to the hose of the bar's sink hose sprayed a misty dew every ten minutes.

Cakes' long, sexy, lotioned ass shined and stretched outside of her poom-poom shorts as she strode across the green living room carpet and placed her bags at the bar. "What y'all doing here?" She looked specifically at me, while pour-ing herself a drink. "What's up, boo? You look-ing kind of snazzy today. Where you off to, a job interview?" she sarcastically asked.

"Naw. I'm off to see the 'wizard' about some muthafucking brains, bitch." I grabbed my crotch like Michael Jackson after his acquittal.

Cakes chuckled. "That was actually funny. Anton, you all sitting up there like you don't acknowledge perfection in your presence, nigga. Hail a prominent ho when you see one, nigga." She bounced her ass off his leg.

"Hail the ho, hail the ho." Anton bent over laughing.

"That's right. My shit is magic on the johnson." She winked at me.

"So what you got over there?" Anton joked. "A bag of tricks?"

"Shit you can't afford on the salary you making."

Anton pulled out a roll of hundreds. "My pockets is fine."

"Pennies, nigga. You ain't getting it like Mack. Ain't that right?" Cakes smiled and looked at me.

"I'm not even in this. Y'all two always going at it. Shit, if I didn't know y'all wasn't stupid, I'd think you two was fucking."

"Yeah, me too," Cocaine said, stepping down the last stair and into the end of the conversation. "But I know that ain't the case, right, y'all? Because there's a rule about fucking the help." He snatched Cakes' bags off the floor and threw them on the couch.

"Hi, daddy. I missed you." Cakes kissed his lips.

Cocaine turned his head and pushed her away. "You must be out of your mind, girl. What, you planning on going out on a date somewhere? What the fuck is all this bullshit, Cakes?" Then he started tossing shit out the bags onto the floor.

"I told you I was going shopping earlier. I can't be wearing repeat outfits when the work come in. I'm not like them other raggedy bitches you got munching and punching the clock, daddy. You know my style—Gots to look good for the customers."

As Cakes bent over to collect the fallen luxury items, Cocaine kicked her square in the ass. I could've sworn I saw a pound of that lotion on her shiny legs jump off her skin. She fell onto the pile of clothing in front of her and quickly turned over. Cocaine never liked anyone talking slick, especially no high-priced, hooker-ass ho. Especially when he was feeding and clothing them.

A tear rushed down her eye. "What the hell is you doing?"

"Get this damn shit off my living room floor, Cakes. You spent all of your allowance money on this bullshit. Get the fuck up to your room. Now!"

Cakes quickly scrambled to her feet and stuffed all the clothing back into the bags. Then she slowly walked up the stairs, rubbing her ass.

Anton and me looked at each other then looked at him.

"What?" Cocaine asked in a tone similar to Raphael Saadiq. "When the day comes I let one of my hoes talk to me like that, it'll be a rainy day in Southern California, you hear that? You give 'em one inch and they'll have you living in your own yard under the fucking gas meter." He sipped his drink. "Y'all muthafuckas know what I'm saying to you? Mack, you the next nigga up. I hope you paying attention. I'm trying to train your ass. You got potential, boy. Don't go letting me down."

Cocaine poured two shots of tequila, one for Anton, one for me. "Y'all niggas have a drink with me." He held up his glass.

Anton told him, "You hard on these hoes, man."

"What, nigga? You need to be following in this man's footsteps." Cocaine pointed to me. "This fool is a pussy magnet. He bring the bitches into work."

Anton was upset. "And I don't?"

"You couldn't bring in the New Year without tripping over last month." Cocaine laughed. "You used to be on point. You slipping."

"What you mean, man? How much money and bitches I brought in last year?"

"That's not the point. It's all about chutes and ladders, baby."

Every now and again, when Cocaine had a little drink in his system, he'd just start making up some mind-boggling-ass phrase then build on it. Sometimes it'd make perfect sense; other times it sounded just as crazy as Gnarls Barkley singing the movie soundtrack for *One Flew over the Cuckoo's Nest.*

Anton asked, "What you mean, *chutes and ladders*?"

"Chutes and ladders, nigga." Cocaine coughed after inhaling deeply. "Rewards and consequences. You always start out on a good path, collecting points, respect, street cred and shit like that—That be the ladders that help you climb to the top of this game. Then you got them chutes—bitch-ass niggas, snitches, and informants, haters. Shit of that nature is the chutes that'll land your ass in a world of consequences. The chutes is the shit that'll make you fall, and it won't have shit to do with autumn. The whole idea of this pimp shit is to keep climbing the ladder until all the mutha-fuckas under you look like ants. This pimp shit be about the constant climb. The trick is to never look down, especially if you afraid of heights, muthafucka, because it's just not about pimping these hoes, it's about pimping the system. You ever lose focus of that, and you'll just be part of some bitch's photographic memory." He released a cloud of London fog.

"So what you saying, man?"

"I'm saying I see your true colors shining through, Ton."

"Yo, y'all is bugging," I said. "I got shit to do, Coke. You straight with that paper." I stood up.

Lately Cocaine had been stressing Anton about his inability to make things happen as he used to. He'd been that way ever since Anton had popped these two auxiliary police officers in Flushing Meadows, Queens a couple of months back. I felt in my gut that Cocaine wanted Ton dead, because his mouth would leak if he ever was caught by the pigs for that murder.

"Yeah, youngblood. We be done. Y'all seen my brother around? I ain't heard from him in a couple of days."

"Naw, man, not me," I said. "I just got out."

He said to Ton, "You, nigga?"

"I ain't seen him in a couple of days."

"All right, whatever. Hit my phone later, Mack," Cocaine said as we walked out the door. "We need to talk."

Chapter Four

Mack

As Sade packed her suitcase for the next day's trip down to VA, I said to her, "Baby, I'ma miss your ass. You know that."

"I'm going to miss you too, but I'll be back soon as I can. I just need to see my mother."

"That's what's up, boo. I know I keep asking, but you sure you don't need me to troop there with you?"

"It's all good, daddy. I got this." She kissed my lips. "Let's go out tonight."

"Baby, I got the meat sitting in the sink already."

"Fuck it. Throw that shit in the fridge. Wherever you want to go."

"Well, I could go for some O.G.'s."

"Ma, I mean a real restaurant, with forks and knives at the table, folded napkins and shit. Hello, may-I-take-your order type shit."

"You asked me where I wanted to eat. That's what I want."

"A'ight, mon. We get the bloodclaat Jamaican food," I said, doing my best Jamaican accent. She laughed.

"Something wrong with you."

We walked into the restaurant and sat. The dreads were in full view seated upon the river of seats rapidly running across the enormous dining room. Ceiling fans spun to combat the outpouring of aromatic heat coming from the kitchen.

"Can I talk to you about something, babe?" Sade said.

"What's up?"

"What do you see in me?"

"Ma, what you want me to say?" I said irritated with a conversation that popped up at least once a week. "You gotta get that esteem up. We been together for a minute now. That should say a lot."

"It does. It really does, but there are these times when I get insecure."

"Like when?"

"Like when you don't come home at night."

"Come on, that's business. We talked about this already, Sade."

"*You* talked about it."

"No. *We* talked about it. I told you that when I'm out, it's because I'm making money. You said you understood that. That's the shit that kills me about y'all females. When a man don't work he a bum, when he work too much he's being neglectful. I mean, where does it end?"

"It's not about you staying out to make your money. I'd never stop that. It's about you playing me like I'm one of them dumb bitches at Phenomenon. Then you wanna smile all up in my face without a single regret."

"What the fuck are you talking about? You tripping." I turned my head to sneeze.

Sade stared at me. "Mack, you can look me directly in my eyes and tell me you not cheating."

I accepted the challenge, staring back with more truth in my eyes than Wonder Woman's lasso. "I'm not fucking around on you, Sade."

"I hope not, Mack. I've been real good to you. I'd do anything you ask me to. I do anything you tell me already. So don't let me find out you doing me dirty or I'll kill you. Word to me." She kissed her fingers.

Did I forget to mention that Sade was a jealous girl, like that bitch New Edition was talking about back in the Eighties?

"Don't play with me, Mack. You better not fuck around while I'm gone."

"Can we eat? The food is getting cold."

Chapter Five

Sade

It'd been a while since I'd been here. Home. VA, baby. There's a lot of bad memories here for me. And not just the thing with my mother's man, Glen. Early on in my life I'd made some bad decisions, just as every young woman will do at some point in her lifetime. And only a fool or a liar will say they haven't. My mother Vivian worked hard her entire life to make a better one for me. My father? Well, I wouldn't even know what that word was if it wasn't in the dictionary. But I didn't give a shit. You learn to cope without.

It did hurt seeing all my other girlfriends hanging out with their fathers when I was a kid, but when I turned eleven I had something better than a father. An older friend. At the time he was thirty-eight. I won't say his name, but around that time he was my best friend. He worked in the same supermarket as my mother and claimed to have been watching me. He said he liked what he saw and that I was mature for my age. To an eleven-year-old that didn't mean too much, until he started buying me things. Sneakers, clothes, food. He taught me how to kiss and make love. In the beginning I was scared of that thing poking out from in between his legs. But once he assured me that everything would be okay, I took a grip of it and learned how to suck my first dick, and swallowed my first nut. I gagged and threw up all on it, and he loved it. He absolutely freaking loved it. It made him happy, and that got me even more open for this man.

Then when he laid me on my back and spread my legs, I peed on him out of nervousness, and he licked his lips. It was so nasty but freaky at the same time. I could only chalk it up to being bored, playing house, or even doctor. And the surgery he performed on me with his tongue that day did something to me. I remember crying and shaking out of control and even momentarily losing focus on where I was at. He later explained to me that it was called an orgasm, a convulsive release of explicit love in the form of a fluid. I didn't understand what that meant at the time.

I knew I wanted some more of that explicitness. Then he introduced me to the act of penetration. Pokemon, before the cartoon ever existed.

We continued that open relationship for years, with my mother's knowledge and approval. She'd say, "You might as well start now with an older man. He'll take care of you in the end. Long as you keep that pussy tight, fresh, and clean. Momma ain't gonna be around forever to care of you."

As I got older, so did he. By the time I was sixteen, my attraction toward him began swinging in other directions. When I broke it off, he actually cried and said I was like his daughter and lover at the same time. He harassed me for the next two years until we finally called the police on him.

I hadn't seen him since. It was weight off my shoulders, and I could now freely venture out and find new love.

But, no matter how many dicks I sucked and fucked, I always got played in the end. All the girls called me ho, slut, and dirty bitch, because I got the guys they all wanted, and the ones they did have all wanted me.

Chapter Six

Sade

I must've had the taxi driver go around the block about six times before I finally got up the nerve to stop. The house looked terrible. There was trash all over the lawn. The paint on the garage was peeling. The hose coming from the backyard was laid out on the sidewalk, still running. I pulled it toward the yard, turned the water off, and rolled it up. A sound from the shed startled me. Glen walked out wearing a stained, sweaty wife-beater. He looked to have gained a few pounds and looked a little on the sickly side. He walked toward me through the overgrown, sun-burnt grass, and sucked the remnants of last night's dinner out of his corner tooth.

"Fuck is you doing here? Thought you was gone for good?"

"Surprise. I'm back. Where's my mother?"

"You think just because you all grown-up now and moved on, you can come back here and talk to me any ol' way you want? I damn near raised you." Glen pulled out a cigarette.

"You mean damn near raped me. You don't got shit else to say to me, Glen. I'm not a little girl no more. You don't scare me, so back off before you regret it."

I walked through the back door and entered through the kitchen. The summer heat attracted flies to the dirty dishes piled in the sink. Food stuck to the plates and stunk up the place. Rolls of flypaper hanging from the ceiling over the sink and entrance to the bathroom collected just as many flies as the ones annoyingly buzzing on their backs in the mouse glue traps on the floor. I could've thrown up. I opened all the windows downstairs and took my bags up to my old room.

My mother called over her music, "Glen." She always loved Earth, Wind & Fire. She'd blast it every Saturday morning when she was house cleaning.

Believe it or not, those are what I considered to be better days. When it was just us. When we was more like sisters than mother and daughter. We'd never be able to get that back again. I slowly opened the door and stood at the entrance. She didn't even look like my mother any more as she swayed back and forth in her chair and looked at me.

"What happened to us, Mommy?" I walked over to her with a hug and some tears. "What happened to you? Why didn't you ever reach out to me?"

She didn't hug me back.

I pulled away and went to turn down the music.

"Don't touch it. What are you doing here?" She coughed. "You still crying about the past? I'm fucked up, Sade. I'm not thinking about no past. I bet if you was never born I wouldn't have this shit. Now I got to live with my mistake."

"Yeah, I'm still thinking about the past," I said. "Shit wasn't—excuse me—things wasn't always like this between us. We used to have fun together. When it was just us there was so much more life in both our lives. We was like sisters."

"I was twelve years old when I had you, Sade. Don't you get it? Babies raising babies. You might as well say we was sisters." She coughed then poured herself a straight shot of Hennessy.

"Mommy, even after all the nonsense you put me through I never once looked back and regretted it, or wished I had a different mother," I cried.

"Does that mean anything to you, Ma? I'm your daughter," I screamed. "Your only child." I knocked her glass out of her hand.

"Yes, it means something," she yelled back. "I'm sick, Sade. You over there feeling all bad for yourself. Look at me"—she showed me the scar from where her left breast used to be before the operation—"I'm dying."

"I'm feeling sorry for myself? Me? Feeling sorry for myself? I don't even know who my mother is anymore, and you can't even remember where it all went wrong. But I do. Yeah, that's right. I do."

"Yeah? Don't you dare start bringing up that Glen-tried-to-rape-me shit."

"He tried and has done it more than once. And you knew it all along. That's when our relationship started to change—when you started looking the other way."

"Well, it was your fault. Who in the hell told your fast little ass to be running around the house half-naked all the time? What I always told you? Sade, put on some clothes, Sade, stop walking around in your nightgown, but you always did like them older men. But you didn't get this one."

"That's how you feel about it? That's what you been thinking? That I wanted that ugly, fat-behind creature out there?" I nodded toward the window facing the yard. "I guess we ain't never going to get back to where we used to be, huh, Ma?"

"I guess we not, so you can just take your sad, crying behind on back to the city. I don't need your support."

"Yeah, Ma," I said wiping the tears coming down my face. "You going to straight sit up here and play me to my face and admit you knew Glen was molesting me? You don't feel no fucking way about that," I yelled, my temperature rising. "You don't feel no fucking way, huh? Then you know what? Fuck you too, bitch!"

I quickly snatched the Hennessy bottle off the night-stand and swung it into the side of her face. She rolled out the chair onto the floor.

"You don't care," I said whacking her head. "I don't give a shit no more either," I cried, swinging to her head.

I beat her until she didn't move anymore. I shook my head out of my frenzy, realizing what I'd just done. "Mommy," I whispered. "Ma." I backed away toward the door.

I opened it, and Glen was standing there carrying a six pack of canned beer.

"You still here? Give these beers to your mother." He looked over my shoulder.

I stood frozen and didn't know whether to run or kick him in the balls.

"What your mother doing over there laying on the floor? Viv," he said, barging past me. "What you done did to your mother?" He kneeled beside her. "Viv." He lifted her head up.

He quickly made a move for the nightstand and pulled out a revolver. "Don't you move." He pointed it at me.

He didn't have to worry about that. I still couldn't believe what I'd just done.

He felt for her pulse, and there wasn't one. "You killed her." He pulled back the trigger with a smirk. "You killed her. That money is mine."

I could see nothing BUT insurance policy all up in his eyes. "It was an accident." I walked over to her corpse, my hands slightly raised above my head. I knelt down and kissed her cheek. Her eyes popped open, and we both jumped back as she screamed horrifically.

"Give me the pillow," I yelled to Glen.

"For what?"

"We can split the money. Hurry up." I covered her mouth and nose with my hand.

"I don't have to split anything. All I have to do is say it was a break-in—after I take your dead ass into the woods and dig a ditch."

"Or you can be an accessory to murder. My man know I'm here. My bus ticket is dated for today. My footprints and fingerprints is all over the place from the yard and those filthy-ass windows. So are yours. Now throw me the pillow."

He tossed it over to me, and I threw it over her face. I pressed down with all of my weight and watched her arms aimlessly flap like fallen angels. Her legs kicked up and down like she was swimming for her life. Her entire body exerted one last burst of ineffective energy then collapsed.

"See, mommy, it didn't have to be this way. All you had to do was love me. What are we going to do with her body?" I asked Glen.

"When night comes I know a place up in the mountains of West Virginia."

"So what are we supposed to do until then?"

Chapter Seven

Mack

Ya know we trap all day (oh) we play all night (oh) Dis is the life of a go-getta (ay), go-getta (ay), go-getta

It was Friday night and this was when Phenomenon bumped the most. Strippers slithered down poles and exercised their rights to be eaten out by paying customers—men and women alike.

And in the club, you see a bad bitch, point her out, oh

The crowd screamed, "Go-getta (ay), go-getta (ay), gogetta (ay), go-getta . . ."

Red siren lights spun around the room, and the thumping music seduced the swaying hips of the go-gettas as they danced laps around the hard dicks of the men that groped and slobbered on their previously sucked titties. Expensive bottles of champagne were popped open and loud talking was the theme for tonight. Everybody was having a good time, just as always on a Friday night. I stood at the bar next to Anton while he did his usual, drink—shots of Jamaican rum.

Ton was bugging though. He had a warrant out for his arrest for two murders, and he was just walking around like shit was funky like that. But he wanted to be that nigga. He wanted to be in the position I was in. He wanted Cocaine to respect him the way he respected me. He wanted that love that dude showed a cat with no initiation.

"So where these bitches at, man? I need to hurry up back to the office."

"She said she'd be here. The bitch don't be faking moves. She'll be here."

A small commotion at the door alerted my attention toward the disturbance. Two banging-ass chicks walked in looking like they belonged up on that stage. Niggaz ran right to them trying to get a dance, or a phone number at least.

"Kim," Ton yelled over the music. "That's her, son. That must be her friend she was talking about."

They both approached smiling. Kim was thick but in a shapely kind of way. Her skin was maple-complexioned, and she was about five eight. Her dimples flauntingly caved in each time she smiled.

Her hair was in some crazy, off-the-hook style
with chopsticks sticking out her bun. Her black
tee-shirt had a pink heart of rhinestones with *I'm a
flirt* scripted in rhinestones over it, the neck of her
shirt exposing the cleavage of her thirty-eight D's.

"Hi." She kissed Ton's lips. "My name's Kim.
This my girl, Joi."

"Told you I'd check it out." She smiled from
behind her glasses.

"Word. We saw you at the gas station," Ton
said.

"Yep. So what's really good, y'all? My girl
said something about making some paper." She
looked at us both.

"That's right," I said. "But we going to talk
upstairs. Ton, grab a bottle of—what y'all drinking?"

"We Henny girls," Kim said.

We sat on the couches in the office and drank
over bullshit conversation, some smoke, and a
li'l sniff-sniff, a controllable habit I'd picked up
from Cocaine when I was locked up north.

"A'ight, y'all. Everybody good now," I said
blowing my nose.

"Chilling," Joi said.

"I know y'all already know there's money out
here. Whatever you got going now is nothing
compared to what I can get you. Ain't near one of

them bitches out there complaining." I pointed out the Plexiglas window overlooking the main floor.

"I'm getting paper without sliding down no poles though. All I do is beat these niggaz in the head all day. Ain't no shame in my game," Kim said.

"Yeah. But is you really getting it like that? How long it take to beat a nigga in the head to come up off some gwop? That shit take a minute. I'm talking about real paper, not no punk-ass, measly thousand dollars."

"I'm not stripping," she said.

"Now, I didn't say nothing about that. I'm figuring like this though, ma. You can do way better than what you doing right now."

"How you figure?"

"You'd always be protected. You wouldn't have to wait for bum-ass niggaz to scope you out or you scope them out. There'd always be paper for you on the regular, not just here and there. If you going to be a pimptress, then you going to need a pimp. And don't take it as the take-all-your-money-and-whup-your-ass kind of pimp, but the kind of pimp that'll always have your back no matter what. The kind of pimp that'll love you more than anyone's ever loved you in your life."

Kim broke out laughing and pushed Joi over on the couch. "You're not serious. You hear yourself? You ain't talking to no little, hungry, desperate bitch. Don't run game, hon. Say what it is you trying to say because, if you ask me, it don't look like you can protect much of anything. You too pretty."

"A'ight. Let me be the manager of your pussy so we can get paid. I can tell your shit's a money-machine. Matter of fact, whether your answer's yes or no, here's a li'l something for both of your time."

I reached into my pocket and tossed two thousand dollars in the middle of the couch and walked over to the surrounding windows "I know that ain't shit, but y'all do what y'all do with that. If you want to see that triple, come and holla back at your boy, a'ight? Y'all can bounce." I sat behind Cocaine's desk, propped my feet up on it, and lit a Newport.

"I'm wit' it," Joi said, putting the money in her Prada purse. "I got this pimp now and this nigga doing me mad dirty. You heard of Stan, right? Over there off Linden Boulevard and down Murdock? He got me holed up in some funky-ass basement apartment. He take all my money except the shit to keep me looking dip."

"I heard of that wack-ass punk," Anton said. "He ain't shit. His name ain't striking no fear in nobody's heart. So what, he got the block popping a li'l something wit' da soda trail? I'll take that nigga's whole shit over."

"Ma," I said, "can you get away from him?"

"Never tried. He's taken care of me since I was fourteen, but I can't stand his ass no more. If you can help me get away from him, I'll ride with you." Joi took off her shades.

"That's what's up then. What's up, Kim? You down or what?"

"Naw, I'm good on that. I don't need no pimp because I ain't no ho. I'm out. Let's bounce, Joi."

Ton told her, "You tripping, Kim."

"Take 'em on down for some drinks, man. Joi, I'ma holla, baby. Call, boo."

Chapter Eight

Sade

I know y'all wondering how I went from visiting my mother to straight murdering her cruel, heartless ass. You heard the shit she said to me, right? That ain't no shit a mother is ever supposed to say to her daughter. To see her stare me right in the eyes and say, "Fuck it, it's your fault he was feeling on your booty. Get over it." Fuck that! The shit just made me spaz. It probably seems irrational, illogical, and unrealistic to y'all, but white kids do the same shit every day. I ain't trying to sit here and justify the shit, but I just don't want nobody looking down on me like shit don't happen sometimes. It's nothing but real life and everyday shit.

It'd been two days, and we still hadn't moved her body. We was too busy keeping a close eye on each other's movements.

"Glen, you expecting her to get up and dig her own grave? The house is beginning to stink."

"Yeah, well, let's just go over this alibi one more time because if shit fuck up, I swear to God, I'll kill you before I go to jail."

"You was out in the yard doing lawn work and you went inside to use the bathroom. From there, you noticed the front door was hanging off its hinges, so you immediately ran up the stairs and that's where you found her. Then someone hit you from behind and knocked you out. When you woke up they was gone, and so was the body."

"So how is we supposed to get the money if she's buried in the woods?"

"Listen, Glen, ever hear of an anonymous tip? Stick to the story. You found her dead."

We waited until nightfall then wrapped her body in sheets and plastic. My stomach churned at the awful stench.

"Get her hand," I said as it slipped out the last opening.

It was ten o' clock, and we figured it'd be better to wait until after midnight, when more people was asleep. I went up to my old bedroom, which once was fully furnished but now reduced to a miniature museum for outdated piles of newspapers, magazines, and old bags of clothing. There was a special hiding place up in my closet where I used to keep my most valuable things—jewelry, money, and the gun my boyfriend gave me for my fifteenth birthday. He told me to keep it for him since he was afraid he'd have to use it on me one day if I ever left him.

I didn't trust Glen at all, and I was praying to God that that gun was still up in that little crawl space. I pulled a chair over to the closet and stepped up on it. I lifted the small covering open with my hand and felt around the inner ledges. I felt around again, and there was nothing. My heart began to beat a little faster, as I gave it one last feel around before my hand gripped the hard, cold handle of the .25 automatic. I stuck it down into my panties and held it in place as I jogged back down the stairs and down into the basement. The guestroom down here was never too snazzy, just barely livable. I laid out across the bed and slipped my gun under the pillow.

"Baby," I said as Mack answered the phone, "you ain't even call to see if I made it here all right."

"Huh? Sade, what's good, ma? My bad. Shit been real hectic today. How your moms?"

After a long pause, I said, "She's good as she can be, considering."

"You a'ight?" he asked, as if he sensed something was bothering me. "That nigga giving you a problem? I'll come down there right now," he said over the loud music in the background.

"No, everything's going to be all right now. I'm feeling a lot better now that me and her talked."

"You sure, Sade?"

"I'm sure, Mack."

"You don't sound like it. When you coming home?"

"I'll be down here about a week. Look, babe, I'm tired. It's been a real long day, and I need me some sleep. Do you love me?"

"You know what's up," he said. Then he disconnected the call.

It was around two o'clock in the morning when I heard feet creeping down the steps. I reached under the pillow and pretended to be asleep. There was three light knocks on the door. I'd forgotten to lock the door. I could hear the knob slowly turn. The smell of hard liquor quickly rushed into the room and crowded my nostrils.

"You's about a killing bitch," Glen drunkenly slurred.

He turned on the light switch. He swayed from side to side, a bottle in one hand, his gun in the other.

I was never gonna be able to pull that shit from under the pillow fast enough, so I laid back.

"Dirty ass, you killed your own mother."

"She deserved it." I sat up on the bed. I was actually feeling no fear.

"Who the fuck is you to be judge? You don't decide shit."

"Glen, you better think about the money. Kill me if you want, but a lot of people know where I'm at. Play around."

"I want that money too." He slowly lowered the gun but kept his hand steady on the trigger. "You know, Sade, you might've thought I was mad when I first seen you today, but that was just my way of showing how happy I was to see you. You know I always loved you." He smiled and stuck his tongue through the space where his two front teeth used to be.

"Fuck you!" I spat on him.

"We used to have some real good times to-gether, baby girl"—he tossed the bottle back—"And I'm sorry for taking it from you those times, but it was your fault. You walked around with that li'l phat ass poking out, just calling a nigga. Then I gotta turn around and go to bed with an old bitch when a younger bitch is right up in my own house? Fuck that! You should've just been giving me the pussy. Then I wouldn't have had to take your shit."

I was too tight for tears and too smart to let my illogical instincts cause me to react in a way that would be detrimental to my health. I could see his dick hardening through his boxers then poke out through the slit. It was nothing special either. He massaged it with his gun in hand and looked directly in my eyes.

"Don't make me make you reunite with your momma tonight, bitch. You take off them fucking clothes."

I slowly began unzipping my pink-and-white Sean John hoody. My breasts popped out soon as the zipper reached my waistline.

"Don't play with me"—he cocked the piece—"Faster."

I leaned back and pulled off the sweats and let them drop to the floor. I watched him as he approached with a smile.

"Everything, bitch." He placed the gun to the side of my head.

He kept the gun to the side of my head and began roughly sucking on my titties. He pushed me on my back and got on top of me. I didn't scream and I didn't cry when he ripped off my panties and powerfully inserted his dick into my dry walls, grunting wildly as he pounded my insides with hate, anger, and aggression.

The bed convulsively shook and hit the wall. "This not good to you," he yelled. "Make a noise like you know good dick." He pressed the gun deeper into my left temple. "Come on," he said, dragging me off the bed by my arm.

When I fell on the floor, he grabbed me by the wrist. "Stay on your knees," he said, pulling his boxers off. His dick pointed at me and stared a bitch eye to eye. He grabbed the back of my head and led me to do what most of us bitches want to do in life anyway—get ahead.

"Auuggh," he screamed, looking up. "Ugghh." He nutted inside my mouth.

I literally drained his soul, and he momentarily lost focus. I quickly cocked back my fist and drove it straight into his balls. He didn't just drop, the nigga tumbled backwards, but still had his hand on the muthafuckin' gun. I darted to the pillow and cocked the .25 the way my ex had taught me.

Just point and shoot! I kept quickly reminding myself. "Take your hand off that shit now, Glen, or I swear to God, I'll kill you. Remember that—I swear to God, I'll kill you?"

He released the gun then balled up into the a fetal position and moaned in agony.

I picked up his gun and kicked him in the balls. "Yeah, look at you now, helpless bitch."

I kicked him in the balls again. "Now, I'ma tell you something. There never was a life insurance policy, asshole. That's a ploy my mother used to attract greedy-ass niggas like yourself. Once word got out she was worth something everybody wanted to be her bodyguard."

"So we killed her for nothing?" he said through drunken pain.

"No. See, your ass so stupid, you never knew my momma had some money tied up into the stocks. It's worth a quarter of a million dollars. I got all her information, so I won't have no problem getting it." I stepped over him carrying both guns. "I was here to figure out a way to get my hands on it." I pulled my sweats and hoody back on. "You just made shit a lot easier."

"So what you gonna do? Kill me?"

"Get up!" I aimed both guns at him. "Get the fuck up!" I yelled. "You don't know how bad I want to shoot you," I said trembling.

My phone chirped. *Bleeeep!*

I ignored it and walked forward as Glen stood with his hands up.

"Sade," Mack said through the phone's speaker. He called again, "Sade."

"You gonna answer that," Glen said. "Helllllp," Glen yelled toward the phone as if he could be heard.

"Nigga can't hear you, stupid. Get up the stairs. Where the keys to your car?"

"I lost them," he said as he reached the top step.

I swung his gun into the back of his head and pushed him into the kitchen. "Where the keys, Glen?"

He pulled the car keys out of his pocket and held them out to me.

"Toss them here," I said, holding my hand out.

After he tossed them, I searched through the set looking for the one to his '84 gold Plymouth.

"All right, let's go." I directed him through the kitchen door into the garage. "Get in the car and drive," I said, pushing the button to open the automatic garage.

The loud humming of the motorized opener momentarily drowned out Mack's voice. After a while he gave up chirping.

I grabbed a shovel off the wall then got into the back seat of the car. Glen cautiously sat behind the wheel.

"Drive," I told him, as the door closed down behind us, and we pulled out the driveway.

"Where we going?"

"Where you think? To dig a hole for a body."

It took all night long, but Glen had finally completed digging the seven-foot grave. He crawled out of the hole and panted heavily. He staked the shovel down in the pile of soil next to the hole and used it to balance his overexhausted body. "Now what." He looked back at the grave.

"Now nothing," I said, aiming and shooting him once, with my eyes closed.

The loud explosion caused by the gun echoed throughout the woods and sent the morning birds into a frenzied panic. They flew through the patches between the green leaves on the tall trees and danced in front of the red rising sun. I ran, following the same trail we'd both traveled to get here, and jumped into his car.

I got onto the West Virginia Parkway and headed to a motel in Richmond. Sirens flashed behind me, and my heart skipped a beat. I looked into the rearview mirror then the driver's mirror. I pushed both guns as far under my seat as they could go. They sped up beside me and accelerated after the green Nissan pushing well over one hundred miles per hour. As my heart slowed down, so did the car I was driving.

I had to pull over on the side of the road for a minute to gather my composure. Traffic was light enough for me to toss both guns far off into the woods. I got back into the car and turned on the radio to my favorite station. I merged back into traffic with a smile on my face as if I'd just gotten away with murder or something.

Chapter Nine

Mack

Cocaine's white SL sat on shimmering chrome twenty-fours outside the chain-link-fenced gate of the park. Mad people shot up peace signs from the basketball court, and ladies young and old approached him with kisses in the lips and cheek as we sat on chess tables in Hollis Park.

"See, young blood—Pardon me." He looked at a potential ho wearing a skirt so short, you could see her bare cheeks firmly exposing themselves. "Mmm, mmm, mmm." He shook his head from side to side. "When you ready to make some money, you holla at me, baby." He smiled.

"I will," she shyly responded and walked away tugging her skirt down.

"What you was saying, man?" I said.

"See there, boy? That right there is gonna be a fine piece of ass one day."

"How can you tell?" I looked at her.

"She only look about sixteen."

"That's when the pussy is the freshest. You control that bitch while she a young ho then when she get older you'll have a faithful ho. Your problem is that you too pretty for your own good. These bitches just ain't gonna listen to you because you a sexy nigga. She not gonna suck your dick every night because you compliment her when y'all together. She's never gonna respect you if you can't take a situation in the chokehold and squeeze the life out of it. A bitch want to feel protected like she did when she lived with daddy. She want a hero."

"A'ight, super pimp," I joked.

"I'm serious. You need to know this because Anton ain't the only nigga slipping, dig?"

"Naw. What you talking about?"

"She's cramping your style. You used to be real hard on these broads. Now you be letting them make you meet their demands, instead of them meeting yours, man. I can't hand this all over to you if you don't have the mindset, baby."

"What? Sade don't got nothing to do with this."

"She got everything to do with it. When was the last time you fucked another bitch besides her? Don't even answer that."

"What about Cakes? She not cramping your style?"

"Fuck a Cake. She's my main investment. That's all."

"You don't be acting like it, yo."

"Anyway, this ain't about her. You need to dead Sade or put her to work. She ain't the prettiest thing, but she sure has a fine body, nice lips. Good for excellent service, baby. You better wake up if you really want this. You got six bitches to look over and whoever else you pull in. Now about that thing with Ton"—he moved closer to me.

"What about him? What thing?"

"The cops he popped, that thing," he said, aggravated.

A shadow over our heads blocked the sunlight, and our reflexes reacted accordingly as the leather orange ball from inside the courts bounced out over the gate and knocked over the two bottles of open Heineken.

"Yo, man," I yelled out standing up.

A six foot seven nigga jogged out the court to retrieve the ball. "My bad."

Cocaine calmly asked the kid while pointing at the sudsy trail of beer, "You gonna pay for that?"

"My bad, man. I just brought a can of soda with my last dollar. I'll see if one of them niggaz over there got it."

"Naw, I want you to pay for it."

"I just told you I'm broke. What you beefing about? It's only beer."

Cocaine swiftly hooked his cane around the kid's ankle and made him fall backwards. As he tripped over and fell on his back, Cocaine began kicking him. Some of his peoples attempted to come to his rescue by hopping and flipping over the gate but quickly did the remix to Juvenile's "Slow Motion" when I produced my burner .

"Nigga, don't you ever in your life disrespect a nigga that been on this earth before you," he said, kicking his stomach. "Somebody got a problem with this?" Cocaine slid his .45 out of his back holster. "Do anybody got a problem?" he asked again, swinging the gun from left to right. "Now," he said, looking down as he placed his joint back in its home, "I'm not one of these little-ass niggaz out here. You test me again and it'll be the last test you ever fail, you understand me?" He pulled the dude to his feet. "Now get the fuck outta here." He kicked the dude in his ass then threw the ball at the back of his head as he sprinted out the exit of the park.

After the crowd dispersed, Cocaine kicked the shattered green glass in his path. "Let's ride, nigga."

"What was that all about?" I asked, while he drove off with my foot still dangling outside.

"Second thing you better remember about this line of business is that it ain't no different than any other. My name is all I have. If you can't keep niggaz from disrespecting me then why a bunch of bitches with aspirations gonna respect you? That boy was out of line. Sometimes you have to humiliate someone to make them humble theyself before you."

"But why you keep telling me shit I already know? You don't have to keep schooling me."

"No, nigga. Apparently I do. Don't be falling in love, youngster. You can't have feelings for no ho then try and commit to one. These bitches will leave Nike tracks all over your forehead, nigga, I'm telling you."

"Not Sade, man. She's a good girl."

"What are you, a fucking idiot? None of them is good. But fuck it, playa, you know some new shit about the game I don't? Then ride with it, homeboy. I'm finished." He headed toward Murdock Avenue. "Now about, Anton . . . he a real rider. He handles his business, but shooting them cops was one of the stupidest things he's ever done. Not the only thing, but the stupidest. When he finally gets caught, he'll talk."

"What? Ton a snitch? Never that."

"You'd be surprised the things a nigga will do when his back is up against the wall. He'll talk, Mack, so he has to go."

"What?"

He stuck up one finger in between us and continued. "Didn't you learn anything while we was locked up? While you was locked up? The prisons is full of nothing but niggas who make deals to save their lives, save themselves from a lifetime sentence. Think about if it was you. Cops get some major case on you and they say, 'Tell me something juicy.' Whatever your charge is, whether it be murder, tax evasion, prostitution or even rape, if what you giving up is bigger than what you got going on, you just might be a free man the same day you was brought in. You understand what I'm saying to you? Pimping is understanding and conquering through reverse psychology."

Cocaine's adamant philosophy on this, that, and the other was sinking in.

Ton was my man, and if Cocaine wanted to kill him or have him killed, I was going to warn him first. At the same time, though dude had been acting mad suspect lately, all edgy and shit, it made me think back to that park incident last week. I shook the shit off.

"So which one of the wolves you going to have take that man's life?" I stared at him awkwardly.

He stared back as we sat in the drive-thru at White Castle. "You."

Chapter Ten

Mack

I'd been ringing Sade's phone off the hook for two days. Chirped that ass and everything. Guess I was going to have to schedule a trip down to VA the next day. I knew she was a soldier and all, but what if that Glen nigga had done something to her? Or maybe I was just bugging.

She probably just wanted to chop shit up with moms undisturbed, I thought to myself as I drove to the mall to meet up with Joi, who was already in the parking lot when I pulled up.

"Yo, what's good, baby?" I said, puffing on a black. "Hey, Mack. So you want to grab something to eat up here?" She got out her car. "Yeah, we can run up in here. They Chinese food is what's really good."

"Whatever. It don't matter to me," she said, adjusting her shades.

We both ate the bourbon chicken and steamed vegetables. Lines from the other food markets reached the tables, violating their three feet of personal space.

I sipped my homemade iced tea. "So how long you been out here doing it?"

"Like I told you before, since I was fourteen."

"How old are you now?"

"Twenty-six. Why? Is that too young?" She smiled before blowing the steaming piece of chicken.

"Nope. You're going to be my piggy bank. We going to make it happen. Now about this nigga, Stan—You don't have to worry about that dude no more."

"Whatever. I'm going where that paper at. Just be real with your words. I don't want dude coming after me."

"Naw," I said, shaking my head. "You don't got to worry about nobody else no more."

"We'll see."

After dinner I dropped her back off at the corner of Stan's house.

She looked around before getting out. "So you sure you gonna take care of his punk ass tonight?"

I waved her off. "Go 'head. I told you there ain't nothing to worry about."

I drove off and speed-dialed Anton.

"Yee-o," he answered.

"Ton, this Mack. Where you at, captain? I ain't heard from you in a minute."

"I'm on Foch Boulevard checking that black-ass nigga, Gordy."

"Yeah? What his ass talking about?"

"Same ol' shit about how he's supposed to be in the position you at. He real hot about that shit."

"Well, fuck it. Ain't shit he can do about it now. Anyway, I called because I'ma need you to be on point tonight."

"With what?"

"That Stan thang."

"Oh, no question, my nigz. Just tell me when and where."

"I hear he be at The Golden Egg every Saturday night. You know that new shit that just opened a couple of months back?"

"Yeah. Now that you mention it . . . I saw him up in there trying to play boss hog, but he all bitch. What's the game plan?"

"You already know what it is."

"You tell Cocaine about this?"

"Naw. He don't need to know. He cool with dude. This is something I need to do and he don't need to know shit. Oh yeah, dawg, there's something else I need to holla with you about later."

"Good or bad?"

"Ain't nothin' nice. You not going to like it."

"So why you can't tell me now?"

"Later," I said hanging up.

Cocaine and Stan wasn't the best of friends, but they wasn't the worst of enemies either. They both respected each other's territory and craft. When either one was short on anything, the respect factor was so great between the two that the other would front whatever was needed. That's how it was with them ol'-school niggaz. There was never an issue of legitimacy when it came to words of honor and contractual handshakes. It was all about respect and the work you put in. There could never be room for jealousy and hate if niggaz could just work together. What they shared now was a rarity in business amongst these new-age pimps. There once was a time when all you had to do was put your trust in God then adapt the rest to a dollar bill. Somewhere along the line a nigga got greedy and wanted everything for himself. He divided the trust, the respect. The dollar was ripped in half and became fifty cents. Two sets of niggaz on opposite sides of the counter waiting to be dropped in the piggy bank. But for every quarter dropped in, it put the next one under. So instead of everybody getting richer, they all died trying. The rest ended up as faded memories from an era now known as forgotten, just like the victims of Katrina.

Chapter Eleven

Mack

"I'm just going in here to talk to the nigga first," I said to Ton as he pulled to the curb of Stan's house in his forest green Acura.

"That nigga ain't about no talking, man. If you ain't no bitch then you don't got shit to say to him is how he see it. You think you fien'in' to walk up in there a shot call? Nigga, please."

"I got this," I said, looking at him.

I walked right up to the door and rang the bell. The light in the bay window flickered on behind the white curtains. Anton slid down in the seat and held his gun by the window.

Stan opened the door and stared me down. He wasn't at all what I'd perceived him to be. I was expecting, you know, a much more intimidating kind of dude, somebody I might have to get the drop on. But dude right here? Look at him, y'all. Hold up. Let me move out the light. Y'all see him? What? He about five foot six, complexion all smoothed out like melted peanut butter with a freckle here and there. See where I'm going with this? I'm sitting up here expecting Jerome's ass to come sliding across the lawn with a mirror because this nigga was straight looking like a bootlegged Morris Day, out here wearing a white silk robe with his name stitched on it.

"What can I do you for, playa?" He flicked on the porch light.

"I'm looking for a lady."

"Only lady here is my wife," he said, keeping his left hand in the pocket of his robe, "and you know you can't have her." He chuckled.

"Your wife, huh." I looked over his shoulder into the house. "You got somebody here with you, playa?" I said.

He looked closer at my face in the light and laughed out loud then pulled his hand out his pocket.

"Cocaine put you up to this, didn't he?" He placed his hand on my shoulder. "Come on in, man. You want a drink or something?"

His entire living room was nothing but glass and mirrors, the coffee table, the grandfather clock, wall-to-wall mirrors reflecting every angle of the first floor's rooms. The carpet was white and looked like freshly fallen snow. A 125-gallon fish tank held a small family of white carp and was supported by a glass stand.

I can't front. I was taken afar. The shit looked like some real official ol'-school shit. All he was missing was some fluffy slippers and *Huggy Bear* tatted across his chest.

"Yeah," I chuckled. "Cocaine sent me," I said, following him into his entertainment room. "He kind of did and didn't."

"Well, which one is it, boy? Did he or didn't he?" He stirred his drink. "You his right-hand man, Flaco, right?"

"Mack."

"That's right." He snapped his fingers. "So talk, man. What you need to talk with me about?"

"Well, remember when you asked me that earlier at the door, I said I wanted a lady, right? That's what I'm here for—one of your ladies."

"Oh, for the night? Not a problem." He pulled down a small photo album from atop his bookcase.

"Naw, not for the night."

"Then what you mean then, nigga? You want a bitch for the week?"

"You mind if I sit on your expensive couch?"

"Something the matter with your ass? Go 'head and squat. Which one you want?" he said, stomping on the floor. He showed me a collection of women, Joi among them. "This right here is a special piece of pussy. If not for the taxes on this house, I'd send her on vacation. But this bitch here keeps the bills paid."

"Yep. That's the one." I smiled. "Joi."

"Oh, you know her?"

"I met her. She told me how you scooped her off the streets when she was just a kid and that you be whupping her ass," I coolly said, looking at him straight mean-mugged.

"What, nigga?" He placed his drink on the bar and cocked his gun, which he'd pulled from under the bar shelf.

"Joi's coming home with me tonight, so tell her to get her shit packed and I'll be out in the front."

"Oh, you must got a army outside. You better, because I got one on standby that'll do a military strike on your ass. I'ma call Cocaine. If he not behind this shit, I'll shoot your ass right now." He turned around for a split second to reach for the phone on the wall.

"Put it down." I quickly shot up holding a .45 from my shoulder holster. "Put it down now." I put a bullet through the phone, shattering it into a million tiny pieces that got lost in the plush carpeting. "Joi, come on up. It's all right." I looked toward the basement.

"You making a big mistake, boy." Stan shook his head.

But *he*'d made the mistake. His big-mouth bitch told me about his safe up in Mount Vernon. He kept it in his ninety-year-old grandmother's basement under six feet of concrete inside a hollow cubby concealed by a trap door. She said he'd been saving since the late '70s and didn't believe in trusting any banks with his money. He wouldn't have to worry about that shit no more.

"So this is how you're gonna earn your rep? By killing me? I'm telling you for the last time—Turn around and walk away. Nobody'll ever have to know about this, not even Cocaine."

"Shut up, nigga." I waved the gun at him. "Joi," I yelled, "let's go."

The basement door slowly opened, and she walked up out of there.

Stan pushed back his processed straightened hair. "Baby girl, you know about this?"

Joi shamefully bowed her head and stayed near the basement door.

"Come on, Joi, you can make your money now. You don't need his ass to manage your career. You need somebody to look out for you. His old ass don't care about you. He old enough to be your daddy."

"You gonna let a stranger kill the man who took your bummy ass off them streets? You got your priorities twisted. When I found you, what was you doing, huh? Yeah. She was eating out the fucking garbage. She was stinking, and I put that dirty, deprived ass in the shower, gave her some soap, and taught her how to clean that filthy little pussy. Didn't I do that shit for you?"

When she didn't respond he yelled, "Didn't I?"

Stan looked at me and pleaded with his eyes. "You don't gotta kill me, man. You can have the bitch. The customers claim she make too much noise anyway. I used to say the same shit before I decided that you'd never get anywhere using your own product." He rubbed his chin and winked at her.

"You don't got to worry about me killing you because I'm not the one who's going to do it." I said to Joi, "Who else in here with y'all?"

"Nobody." She sniffled. "We here alone."

I pointed the .45 to his head. "Give her the keys to the safe, man."

"All right, big man. How about this? Fuck you and I ain't telling you shit. You not going to kill me. Cocaine told me all about you. You don't do shit, and you don't make nothing go 'round. Did he tell you that, Joi? Why don't you tell her about your little initiation, Mack?"

"Shut up!"

"Naw, partner. If you gonna be 'captain save a ho' then she need to know who's saving her. You better think about that shit." He pointed at her. "When I come to get him you'll be next."

"Well, you know what, Stan?" Joi said, getting this boost of courage out of thin air. "Anything gots to be better than living here with you. What the fuck you do for me? Not a damn thing."

"So what you going to do, bitch—let the next man sell your pussy? You going to let him sell the pussy that I helped you rear? That pussy wouldn't be worth a fuck if I didn't rear it. You was homeless, and I took you in, you forgetful ass."

"Took me in and what?" She walked closer to him. "Took me in and what?" she yelled, balling her fists.

He smirked. "Took you in and loved you just like a stepdaughter."

"Give me the gun, Mack." She calmly extended her hand.

"What?"

"I want to kill him. You hear that, you fucking bastard? I'm going to kill you, just like you did my childhood."

"Aw, shut the fuck up, Joi. Now tell your little friend there to just pass me the gun. If he was going to do shit, he would've done it soon as he walked in. He's a bitch. And this the dude you think going to protect you? Why you think he ain't mentioned that initiation thing to you?"

"Shut up, man!" I cocked the bitch.

He began chuckling. "Yeah, Joi, his initiation was special, wasn't it, Mack stick?" He laughed and reached for his drink.

I shot him once in the chest, and his body slammed against the brass railing of the bar and slumped to the floor. I stood over him and emptied the entire clip. I reached into his robe pocket and came up with a single key on a ring. "Is this it?" I said, holding it up.

"I think." Joi was shaking.

"Look at the shit—is this it?"

She examined it a little closer this time. "Y—yeah."

"Let's go." I grabbed her by the wrist and ran out to Ton's running Acura.

"Y'all good?" he said screeching off.

"Naw, nigga. Drive. Get us the fuck out of here now," I said breathing heavily.

Joi sank into the back seat and hollered hysterically.

Ton hit the corners of the block like he was driving brake-free. "What the fuck happened in there?"

We raced down the through the streets, leaving a thick trail of exhaust and late-night curiosity. Residents started opening up they doors, and some was even on they cell phones before we ever passed they house.

"You know where we driving to?" Ton said, looking around for pigs.

"Get on the first parkway you see. I don't care which one."

"You better care, nigga. I'm wanted, remember? Think of something." Ton asked, "Yo, what's up with your girl Kim's house?"

"Nothing's up," Joi said. "She your people too. Call her."

"Everybody just be calm. I'm cool now," I said, recomposing myself. "Ton, let shorty stay with you tonight. Sade suppose to be coming home."

"Mack, what happened?"

"I killed him."

Anton slammed on the brakes, and the car did a 360.

Chapter Twelve

Sade

With Glen and my mother dead I could have all that money for myself. I parked Glen's car in an Eckerd's parking lot and stepped out with a duffle bag filled with money. The other half of the money was locked away in an untraceable CD account at a bank my mother used to work for. I found the PIN in her drawer taped to a side panel. I memorized it and flushed it down the toilet after shredding it.

I boarded the Greyhound bus and walked to the back.

"Good evening," the bus driver said. "My name is Wilson Norman, and I'll be your driver for the duration of your journey. We'll be making stops in Baltimore, Delaware, Newark, and our final destination, Port Authority in New York City. Passengers, please be wary and courteous of the person sitting next to you and turn down your phone or radio. If you have headphones, please use them. The time now is six P.M. Estimated time to New York, six and a half hours. Thank you, and please enjoy the ride."

The lights dimmed, and the bus beeped as it reversed out of the port. I looked out the window at a man waving orange sticks and wearing an orange mesh vest. He directed the driver into the street, then we moved forward. The bathroom door swung open and closed as we ran over the first few bumps in the street before turning onto the parkway, released strong combined scents of shit, pee, and Pine-Sol. Complaints of the wretched smell traveled up the narrow aisle of the bus and to the back again.

I drowned out the annoying chatter around me by closing my eyes and shutting off my ears. But how could I really sleep? I'd just murdered my mother, and her boyfriend the rapist. I didn't know why I was tripping though. I went down there wishing I could kill him. I just couldn't live another day knowing that he thought he'd gotten away with rape. What irony. My mother just happened to be saying the wrong things at the wrong time and I blacked. So fuck it! Don't let anybody tell you that it's hard to kill because, under the right circumstances, you'd be surprised at the things you'd do. I did what I had to do, and I wasn't done yet.

Chapter Thirteen

Mack

I awoke to Sade's warm tongue kissing the left lobe of my ear, the street light peeking through the folds of the Venetian blinds.

"You just getting in?"

I sat up.

"What time is it?" I looked at the digital display on my DVD player.

"A little after two," she said, hugging me.

"I missed you."

"Me too. Why you didn't chirp me? I would've came and got you from the Port Authority."

"It's okay. I needed that extra time to clear some things in my head."

"How'd it go? You work things out with mom dukes?"

"Yeah, we good now."

"A'ight. So when you going to see her again?"

"No time soon. That chapter of my life is closed now."

"Glen didn't have shit to say?"

"Baby, don't worry about none of that." She kissed on my chest. "I'm home now and still missing my man, even though he's sitting right by my side."

"Sade, I got something to talk to you about. You tired, or you want to chop it up in the morning?"

"It's morning now. Make some coffee and I'll be all ears."

We walked into the kitchen, and I turned on the thirteen-inch television sitting on the counter next to the microwave. Sade put the coffee on and placed the mugs on the table before us.

"You know how I been talking to you about Cocaine pushing me up the ladder, right? Well, that time is almost here. I'm about to come up," I told her.

Sade knew that there was always a catch to everything I said. "How?"

"Pimping."

"What? Pimping? You? No way. Not while I'm living here, you won't. Why you got to be pimping? You already helping run Premonitions. You around bitches all night."

"We need money, babe. I mean, we got dough, but we need more. You want to just live satisfied for the rest of your life, or do you want to be totally over-fucking-whelmed in wealth?"

"I'm working, and you doing your thing. We good. Why you letting this nigga Cocaine pimp you? Don't take that the wrong way, but he playing you for a fool. I only met him once, and I know he not looking out for you."

"Cocaine a good dude."

"Why he always so good to you? You special or something? Shit, Mack, you don't find it odd you the only nigga down that ain't been initiated yet? He got you brainwashed or something?"

"Nobody got me brainwashed, Sade. It don't take a genius to figure out that no matter how much money you got or how much you make it's never enough."

"You must think you talking to one of them bum-ass tricks up in that bar. Only a dumb bitch would let her man pimp some bitches and think he not going to be fucking them."

"Come on now, baby. You know how I get down. When it comes to business, that's what it strictly is. I'd never let no other bitch come between what we got."

"And what we got, Mack? Huh? What we got? You acting like I don't know you fuck other bitches. You don't know how to hide shit. You know how I know you be lying about shit? Because when you start telling me bullshit your eyes start blinking mad fast and you stutter."

"You beefing? You ain't answered your phone but one time since you was away. Who's to say you and Glen didn't fuck and make up for ol' times' sake?"

I never saw the slap coming. All I felt was the impression left by her hand stinging on the side of my face.

"Fuck you, Mack. That was low, and you know it." She stormed out the kitchen back into the bedroom.

"So what happened then? Why you wasn't answering the phone?" I said, trying to psychologically revert the conversation in my favor.

"Don't even try that shit. We not even talking about that right now. That ain't even come out your mouth until you got backed into a corner. You can be real and truthful with your OPT homies, but you can't be that for me. What the fuck is the matter with that picture?"

"Know what, baby," I said, putting my hands on her shoulders, "you had a long weekend and bus ride home." I kissed her forehead. "Why don't we get some sleep and talk about this later tomorrow?

"Whatever. My response is not going to change."

"All right, ma." I pulled back the sheets on her side of the bed. "I know. Come on and lay down. You mad excited right now."

I sat on the side of the bed and ran my hand up and down her back, and she dozed off instantly.

Chapter Fourteen

Mack

Me and Ton was out shooting the rock inside a park in Hollis, Queens. Joi stood by the chain-link fence drinking bottled water, her legs shimmering under the baking sun. She wore a white sports bra under her black wife-beater, and open-toed black sandals. And every once in a while she'd take off her tan straw hat to fan herself.

Ton fell on the red-and-green asphalt. "That's a foul, nigga. Get up and cut out the theatrics." I laughed and pulled him from the ground. "I'm shooting three." He frowned, wiping sweat from his forehead. "You shooting your mouth. What you talking about three? Your foot was inside the line."

"What? Nigga, I was fading away."

"Just like that lie. It's just faaaaading away," I said, slowing waving my hand. "Shoot two." I bounced the ball to him behind the foul line.

"What's up, Joi? You want some of this?" I said, stealing on Ton then dribbling the ball between my legs. "I'm taking you to Jersey." I spun on him then teardropped it into the net. "You can't fuck with me, dude. Call me when you're older, kid. Game over." I slapped his ass.

"Fruitcake." He walked over to his bag to pour himself a drink.

"You don't think it's a little too hot to be drinking?" Joi asked.

"I like hot." Ton gulped down the shot of Christian Elijah vodka.

My man Ton. I didn't give a shit what Cocaine was talking. I was going to let Ton know what the deal was. At least he'd have a heads-up. Besides, I ain't no killer. I might be a flirt and a pimp and a good liar when necessary, but surely not a killer.

"Yo, Ton, I need to talk to you. First, let's raise the fuck up out this park. You really bugging, man. You out here fucking around and you a wanted man. Is you trying to get caught? They're going to kill you."

"Not as long as I got my main man, Mack Rock, next to me. I know you got my back, right?" He took another shot and wrapped his arm around my shoulder.

"Mad early and this dude getting twisted already." I grabbed the ball and tossed it into the back of my Suburban.

"I'ma drop this cat off at his crib then me and you got business to talk about," I said to Joi.

"The apartment you got me is tight. I've never had my own place before. I mean, a room here and there for rent, but that shit got everything," she explained from the back seat.

"Hey, I'm glad you like it. That's a hook-up from my man. You don't got to pay shit. All you got to do is come to the bar every night and rake in the customers. I'm taking you places, ma. You believe me?"

"Whatever. Just remember how you getting there. I ain't never going to tell nobody. I don't need that shit coming back on me, so that's your credit right there when it come down."

"Ton. Ton, man," I said, shaking him awake. "You home, bruth. Get your drunk ass in the house." I pushed him out the car. "Get in the front, Joi. Think you riding in a limo or something?"

"Bye, Ton," she said as he stumbled up the steps to his mother's home, where he stayed in the basement. "Why you be acting like that to him? Ain't he your man?"

"He know I just be playing with him. Yo, don't do that no more."

"Do what?"

"That shit right there—questioning me. We not about to get this shit off on the wrong foot. I'm running the show."

"Okay, I got you." She looked out the window.

"So you going to invite me to your new place or what?"

"Oh, you finally coming to test the product? That's what's up."

"That's right, that's what's up."

Chapter Fifteen

Anton

Mack this, Mack that. Mack can suck my dick. That's what I think about him. He a cool cat and all, but he a wannabe. He always saying we menz, but I met him through Cocaine way before I met his ass. When I was coming up, Cocaine's name really was out there, and he was looking out for a young nigga. My moms and pops didn't take well to a li'l nigga like me hanging out with the neighborhood pimp, but they couldn't control me though. I was fourteen years old and did what I wanted. At that time I was what the kids of today is trying to be—emulators. I wanted to be the hustler of hustlers. I wanted to have bitches falling all over me, be able to pay the pigs off any time I wanted them to turn their heads and look the other way. Instead I did a three-year stretch in prison behind drug and robbery charges.

When I got released I was kicked down into the basement of my mother's house next to a washing machine, where I slept on a fucking air mattress. All the street dreams I had of becoming something made a nigga succumb to absolutely nothing. Cocaine knew exactly what he was doing when he decided to play big brother. He preyed on niggaz that thought no one at home cared. From there he'd have you doing all kind of shit for him and have you looking at him like he daddy, like he got love for you and shit just because he flashed some money.

As a young nigga the only thing you thinking about is how many pairs of sneakers you going to buy to impress the bitches. And this nigga thinking how many one-dollar bills he gotta spend to keep impressing you. Not many. Because just like a ho, you caught up in the midst of an illusion. And it don't take no magician to show your silly rabbit ass that you just another dumb-ass nigga pulled from his hat, just like the rest of his tricks.

After me and Cocaine started drifting apart, me and his younger brother Gordy became cool. Gordy was an evil, black muthafucka who hated on everybody and everything a nigga had or did better than him. He was another dude put a step under because of Mack. He hated that and swore one day he'd murder that nigga, if it was the last thing he did in life. Why his brother, his own flesh and blood, didn't love him the way he loved Mack? What part of the game is that? There was just more niggaz that deserved his stripes.

I answered my cell, "Hello."

"Nigga, this Coke. Come out. I'm in front of the house."

I wobbled out the back door and to the passenger door. "What's up, man?"

"You drunk, man? Get your ass in the car. We got a problem." He locked the door after I got in. "Where's Mack?"

"He with that bitch, Joi. Why? What's up?"

"Stan is dead. Somebody shot him in his own house the other night. The bitch he had up in there is gone. She might have something to do with it. We need to find her before she have them fucking pigs swarming the block."

Only thing that was keeping me alive was the fact that this fool didn't know Joi was the missing bitch. He tried chirping Mack again, but he got no answer.

"We need to go for a ride, Ton."

With the tone in his voice I already was regretting not bringing my jump-off out the door with me. "Where we going?"

"For a ride, nigga. What? You got a reason to be nervous about something?"

"Naw. I just promised my moms I'd do some shit around the rest."

"Don't worry, you'll be back in time."

We drove for about an hour in complete silence. I looked out my window the entire time. We pulled in front of a house in the Bronx. The lawn had blades of grass leaning over, and the streets was littered with pothole gravel, empty soda cans, and pages from the *New York Post*. The garbage cans overflowed with old diapers and black plastic bags. Old sneakers hanging by their strings swung back and forth on the almost-stripped telephone lines. A white pit bull with black and brown patches viciously snapped his jaws through the spaces between the rusty, white iron gate.

"Who live here?" I said getting out.

"This where I keep Cakes when I need a break from her."

I looked up and down the street and didn't see anything that remotely resembled a setup, so I followed in his footsteps, just as I'd always done, and waited as he searched his ring for the right key to the door.

"Cakes, it's me." He banged. "Open the door."

"This not even how you move, man. What's going on?" I took a step back.

"Why you acting so suspicious? What you done did?"

"I ain't did shit." I continued to back toward the sidewalk.

The front door opened, and Cakes stepped out. "I didn't hear the door at first," she said, moving out his way.

"Come on, nigga." He said waiting for me.

Skeptical as I was, I slowly crept inside anyway. I walked to the middle of the sparsely decorated living room. "What's good, Cakes?"

"Hey. What's good with you?" she answered, with a warning in her eyes.

I didn't realize how much of an asshole decision it was to come up in here until I felt the blunt force of a hard object strike the back of my head. I heard Cakes scream and then six sets of feet began stomping and kicking me in the stomach and face. It was members of OPT, orchestrated by Cocaine to beat the opera out of me.

One of them put a knee to my neck, and Cocaine knelt beside my face. He said to me, "Tell me why I'm not trusting you right now, boy. You kill two pigs, and you still walking the streets without a care in the world. Why is that?" He snapped his fingers, and this dude applied extra pressure to the back of my neck with his knee.

"Why you trippin' on me for? I ain't did shit. All I do is move the work and collect the bitches, man. I'd never turn on you."

"I don't know why I'm not believing you."

"If I was snitching, do you think I woulda taken the ride all the way out here with you?" I gasped in pain.

"I don't know, but just in case you get any ideas of snitching to get an easier sentence, this is your first and last warning." He slapped me in the face. "Let 'im up," he said to the dude. "I don't wanna have to kill you, Anton. I love you like a son." Cocaine held the side of my face like a father would his own son's when having a man-to-man. "We been in this for a while together. Don't let me have to bury you."

That's when I knew it was going to be either me or him. And if he knew like I knew, instead of messing around, he'd play like Roy Rogers and slooooow down. Maybe he thought because the team was strong that I'd pussy up. I'd play the part for now though.

He opened the front door. "I'll see you tonight at the club."

Chapter Sixteen

Sade

Working for the bank made it a whole lot easier unloading all that money into my account. Over the next couple of months I just added a little more to it each week. I never dressed any different and didn't spend a dime.

I was in the back office eating lunch with a co-worker, when my supervisor walked in with two detectives. "Sade," he said, "these two gentlemen would like to speak with you." He nodded his head at my co-worker to leave.

I stopped eating my bag of chips. "Who are they?"

"Can we have a moment of your time, miss?" The tall red-headed detective looked down at his black leather-padded memo book. "Sade Watkins—is that you?"

"Sir," the second detective said to my supervisor, "this is a private matter."

"Oh, sorry," he said and quickly closed the door.

"I'm afraid we have some very bad news for you, Miss Watkins," the tall redhead said. "Your mother's been murdered. You're the only living relative we've been able to contact."

"Oh my God." I covered my mouth and put on a tear show. "Wh-wh-what happened?"

"Break-in. She must've startled them," the other shorter detective said. "They beat her, then smothered her when she didn't die."

"I was just about to go and see her next weekend," I cried, my head buried deep inside my folded arms.

"Well, the funny thing about it, Sade, is that you were there a couple of months back. It was slick of you to use a different location and credit card, but the one thing you didn't count on was the camera in the taxi. You want to discuss this back at the station? Detectives from Virginia are there waiting for you," continued the short officer.

"Taxi? Cameras? Naw. My mother is dead and you're accusing me of doing it?

"The film is dated, Sade, and there's even more proof."

I stood up. "I want to see my lawyer."

The short detective said, "Please place your hands behind your back."

"You have the right—"

"I know all that. Can I at least make a phone call?"

The redhead anchored me along by the chain of my cuffs. "When we get there."

"Can you please put my jacket over my hands? I don't need to be anymore embarrassed than I am right now."

"No, you don't get an option. Please follow the detective, miss," the redhead said.

"Sandra, call Mack for me and tell him I got arrested," I said to my co-worker.

"Excuse me, detective," my supervisor intervened, "can I ask what she's being charged with?"

Commotion erupted in the office as the bank tellers all turned to me as I left with my head down.

"Murder."

I sat in a holding cell waiting to be handed over to the Virginia authorities. I was taken out and brought into the interrogation room. My lawyer was there, but there wasn't much he could do for me. But he did have a good lawyer friend in VA to defend me.

"Are you all right, Sade?" he asked.

"No, I'm really not. I don't even know what I'm doing here. They're talking about some tape and an extra surprise. What the fuck, Donald? I hope your friend can help me."

He adjusted the rubber band around his ponytail and wiped perspiration from his brow. "What happened, Sade? Can you even account for your whereabouts on the dates in question . . . because this isn't looking good for you at all. I can tell you right now that if you're found guilty you could face up to twenty-five years to life. You don't want that for yourself, nor do I." He reached out for my hand.

"I can't remember."

"That's definitely not a good thing because the evidence against you appears to be airtight. You have to tell me exactly what happened to your mother," he said, removing his eyeglasses and cleaning them off with a napkin.

"Did you see a tape?" I asked.

"No. Actually, I didn't. They're trying to use reverse psychology on you to fess up. I don't even think Virginia taxi cabs have cameras installed in their cars, so you do have that in your favor. The bus ticket and your whereabouts is an entirely different story. I'll ask you again—Do you know anything about your mother's murder?"

With a straight face, I said, "No."

"Okay. I believe you. We're going to get through this. My friend is very good at what he does. Have you spoken with your boyfriend yet?"

"No, I haven't."

"I think it'd be best if you call him now before they extradite you back to Richmond."

"Do you think you can get them to loosen these cuffs some? Where they think I'm going to run to?"

As usual I couldn't get in contact with Mack. I chirped him, rang the line, left four messages, and still nothing.

The arresting detectives arrived in from VA and read me my rights all over again. All I could think about as the detectives slowly walked down the aisle of the chain-link fence was jail time and how my man was nowhere to be found. His mind probably wasn't on me anyway. All he ever thought about was that Rolls Royce money.

They really didn't have anything on me except a bus ticket. *I can't do life in prison.* I could always plead temporary insanity if necessary. Maybe if Mack had been home a little more I'd have never gone out there.

Everything felt as it was moving in slow motion. It was so hot outside, and the only wind blowing was the exhaust from my erratic breathing. Not only because I was being arrested, but the fact that when I really think about it, Mack ain't never been there for me when I needed him the most. Never ever home, and sit right up there and tell me he ain't fucking other bitches. I got that money for us and killed my mother for me. Does it bother me now? I don't know, but I might just have the rest of my life to think about it.

Even though I was in cuffs, I struggled with the two detectives as they tried to push me into the back seat. One of them lost their grip, and I swung my shoulder into the other detective. He stumbled back and the other D grabbed me by the back of my neck.

I screamed and pushed myself backwards, and he fell on top of the hood of their car.

My adrenaline rushed as I tried to run. They both grabbed me and slammed me against the car, not once, not twice, but five times. My body was exhausted, and all I could do was scream long and loud. "Flynnnnnnnnnnnt!"

The short and stocky D opened the door and kicked me inside by my ass and slammed the door shut. I was flat on my stomach with my hands behind my back. They both got in and waved to the crowd of witnessing officers, who laughed, smiled, and gave thumbs-up to another job well done, beating up on a black woman.

We drove off slowly, almost parading down the street as onlookers stared me down in the back seat.

Chapter Seventeen

Mack

I dropped off Joi at her house and was about to follow her inside when I saw seven missed calls on my phone. The numbers all was blocked. No voice mail neither. At the time I wasn't thinking it could be Sade. I called her job, and Sandra gave me the rundown. When she said Sade was being accused of murdering her mother, I didn't believe it. I went to the police station that sent out the Ds and asked for them by the names displayed on the cards that they'd left at the bank.

"Yeah. Are you holding a Sade Watkins?" I said to a young-looking officer at the front desk as other officers and Ds dashed back and forth with coffee, donuts, and prisoners.

"Who is that you're looking for?"

"Sade, man. Sade Watkins." I looked over his shoulder at the small holding cells. "Is she back there?"

The cocky son-of-a-bitch said to me, "And you are?"

"That doesn't matter. If I ask for someone and they're not a minor, then there is no reason why you should be asking me anything." I slapped the desk.

"You do that again and your ass will be arrested for attempted assault against an officer. "Bobby." He turned to the passing D on the way to his desk.

"Yeah. What's up, Chris?" He said, sipping a steaming mug of coffee.

"The girl you and Jeff brought in earlier, she still here?"

"Who's asking?" He stared at me through his clear, crystal-blue eyes of hate.

"Me. She's my girl."

"Oh shit. We was wondering when you'd show up. Come on in." Chris opened the gate leading to the twelve-foot-long desk.

We walked to his desk and sat opposite one another.

"Can I get you some water? A coffee?"

"Duke, I'm good. What happened to my girl?"

"She's been extradited."

"For what?"

"Holy shit," Detective Jeff said. "Mack, aka Eric Williams."

Detective Jeff was the reason I went to prison. He was right there in court every day waiting on my conviction for that bullshit. Not only that, but I fucked his daughter when we was in high school. Everybody knew she was a cop's daughter but was too scared to holla. Me, being the flirt that I was, finessed her right in the girl's bathroom. The silly bitch ended up pregnant, even though we had protected sex. Daddy forced her to abort immediately, promptly, efficiently, and any other kind of -*ly* he could think of, because wasn't no way in the world he was going to stand for no half-breed, mulatto-ass, cross-color, tar baby running around in white face. His father would have never stood for it, and his father's father surely wouldn't have went for it neither.

Detective Jeff took a personal interest in my miniscule criminal career as I got older. Every time I turned around, he was in my face. The final spin flung my ass right into jail, arrested by yours truly, Detective muthafucking Jeffery Cunningham.

"You two old buddies?" Bobby asked.

"Oh sure. Me and this kid go way back. Like to my daughter's abortion." He frowned. "But that's a story for another day. So when'd you get out, Mack? I ain't heard much about you. You on the straight and narrow now?"

"Hold on"—Bobby slapped the table. He smiled. "Muthafucka, Jeff, you know who this is? Solomon Ivory's boy."

"Goddamn. I'll be a son-of-a-bitch. Mack, what the fuck is you doing in here, homeboy?" Jeff said. "We got a long case against you and your little crew, OPT. You got one old man leading a bunch of wild-ass monkeys."

"Man, when I walked in here nobody knew who I was. Now y'all playing 'place that face.' I don't know shit about what you talking." I folded my arms across my chest.

"But you know about Anton, right? Yeah, we know you know something about that. Where's he at?" Jeff said.

I shot up out the chair to my feet. "This is not what I came here for."

Jeff pushed me back to the chair. "Sit the fuck down."

The constant run-of-the-mill police chatter suddenly halted, and the water from the cooler suspended in mid-flow. Jeff's cheeks turned red, and his heartbeat pumped through his shirt.

"Jeff . . . your blood pressure. Relax." Bobby stood and placed his hand on Jeff's shoulders.

Jeff pointed his finger in my face. "This li'l fuck right here is going to give me something."

"I'm not going to be able to control him much longer. Give us something," Bobby said.

"I don't know shit. I'm just here to find out where my girl is."

"Fuck you, Mack! You're the same arrogant, pompous, asshole you were when I first arrested you. I'll be there again when you get convicted. Get the fuck out of my station. Your bitch is in Virginia. You figure out which part, smart guy," he said, storming off toward the men's bathroom.

"So that's it?" I looked at Bobby. "Just VA, huh?"

He passed me a card from the Virginia State Police department in Richmond.

"Good looks," I told him on the way out the gate.

"That wasn't a favor, I'm just doing my job."

When I got outside, my truck was getting towed for being in a police parking spot. I ran to the driver and banged the side of his door. "Yo, I just came out of there," I said, pointing to the station.

"Are you a cop?" the driver asked. An unshaven white man with dusty, shoulder-length hair and crusty yellow teeth, he was wearing blue denim overalls with white pinstripes and could've stood about three or four months in the gym.

"No, I'm not a cop."

"Then get the fuck away from the truck, man. This is a police-issued vehicle, so it'd behoove you not to touch it again." He stepped out chewing his toothpick. He walked around to the back of the truck to be sure the locking gage was secure. He pushed the black lever up, and the other down.

"Look, man, I don't have time for this. How much you want to take my truck off there?"

He looked around, even turned around, looked back at me, and scratched the rough bristles on the side of his face.

"Come on, man, tell me something."

"Two hundred."

"No doubt." I gave him two hundred-dollar bills.

As I pulled off from the station, a blue Nissan Maxima with tinted windows pulled up on my driver's side at a red light. The passenger window rolled down no more than three inches, enough for me to catch a glimpse of the gun sitting on the eggshell-white seat. The driver beeped the horn long and hard then dipped off in and out of traffic when the light turned green.

My phone suddenly rang through my hands-free system, and I jumped in my seat, still trying to piece together what that horn shit was about. I looked down at the police card. "Spit it."

"Mack. Yo, yo, Mack," Ton said, almost in a panic.

"Ton? Where you at, man? What's good?"

"I told you Cocaine wanted me dead. He took me all the way out to the BX, and him and some new wolves pounded my ass out. I don't know why that nigga think I'm talking to the cops."

"Where you at, nigga?"

"I'm on some low shit right now. I don't want nobody to know where I am."

"That shit's going to look suspect, Ton. Shit, you been running around all this time not caring about the pigs, but you worried about Cocaine's ass? Fuck that, Ton. Show your face. You always talking this 'earning-stripes' shit. What kind of hood example you setting for the other niggaz?"

"I did what I had to do to get in. Why he trying to kill me?"

"He was just trying to scare you, man. Look, ain't nothing going to happen to you far as he's concerned. The law is an entirely different story."

"I ain't worried about them muthafuckas, but OPT, Cocaine, man, they'll murder me and my momma."

"Stay where you at for now. I'll come and get you in the morning, and we'll go work it out with him, all right, nigga?"

"You sure it'll be cool?"

"Yo, what I say?" I said to him, beeping my horn at a sexy, middle-aged woman driving a platinum Jaguar convertible.

Chapter Eighteen

Anton

It was my night to hold down the fort in one of the ho houses, three bedrooms upstairs and two in the basement. I was there to collect the paper, while the other wolves made sure the bitches didn't get jerked or robbed. This was one of the houses Cocaine had given power to Mack to run—the house I should've been running. Instead I was acting like a fucking doorman, and Mack was out fucking and recruiting in the field. He was even beginning to act different, now that he was making more money.

And that Stan incident just went to his head. He ain't never kill nobody in his life, and now because he did, he gangsta. It made me sick to see these bitches just falling all over him not knowing that his rep was bogus. It ain't what you did, but how long you do it for. I was really starting to hate that nigga, but I had to be cool with him until he got that spot. Then you gonna see how I pimp and shoot.

Anyway, it was another regular Saturday night, and traffic was controlled by appointment only. Someone came in asking for Joi, but she wasn't here. I know she wasn't at the club. So where else would she be? With that nigga Mack. He fucking up the money with that bullshit. Maybe if I told Cocaine that, he'd sense my loyalty to him.

Gordy walked up the steps of the basement. "Where that bitch, Mack?"

"I don't know. He suppose to be at Phenomenon."

"Cocaine looking for him. This nigga ain't been answering his phone. You heard from him today?"

"Naw, man, not since yesterday."

"Oh, you mean when my brother pounded you out? He would've never done that to Mack, yo. I know that shit gots to have you feeling some sort of way."

"What I'm gonna do, Gord? The whole team think I'm a snitch. The shit is real fucked up. I can't make no real moves."

"Son, you suppose to be top dog. Fuck that! I'm suppose to be top dog. My own blood love that bitch more than he love me. His ass about to be exposed soon though, I promise you that. His fucking day is coming."

Cakes walked out the top-floor bedroom and held the banister as she came down the stairs.

"What's up, Cakes?" Gordy sipped from his can of Olde English 800 and licked his lips.

"Hey, nasty." She smiled and headed to the bathroom.

I said as I massaged my crotch. "She's a bad bitch."

Cakes said, "Anybody heard from Mack? He promised to pick me up."

"Ain't nobody thinking 'bout that punk," Gordy said to her.

"Ill. Why is y'all hating?" she said, pulling her purse strap over her shoulder.

"Where you going?" Gordy said.

"I been here since one this afternoon. It's eleven now. I'm out." Cakes pushed her tips deep down into her tight jeans. "I'm going outside to wait on him."

There was something else. Cocaine didn't like nobody looking at Cakes, much less driving the bitch home, but Mack had these special privileges.

Shit shut down about three in the morning. Cocaine pulled in front of the house by himself half-bent. He and his brother hugged at the door. Then he stood in front of me. My swollen right eye displayed him in a blurry vision. I squinted and stuck out my hand to extend dap, and he pulled me in and embraced me tightly.

"I'm sorry, boy, but you can't trust nobody. You know how the shit go, don't you? You understand, right?"

"Yeah, man, I understand."

"You took that beating like a soldier—That's why you roll with me. We all need to have a sit-down real quick. Where's Mack?"

"He took wifey home. She said you told him to."

"Shit. I forgot about that. Fuck it then. This is some family shit I need to say in front of everybody. I'll get in touch with Mack tomorrow. You got something for me?" he asked.

I handed him the night's intake, and he broke me off a li'l something. He passed Gordy his cut and stepped.

"See this"—Gordy held up the wad of money— "This is bullshit. Mack is stopping me and you from seeing the paper we used to see. What you think we should do about that?"

"What you trying to say?"

"What the fuck you think I'm trying to say? That nigga gotta go, unless you like putting down payments on shoestrings."

"You wanna murder the nigga?"

"I'm not the only one. Mad niggaz is venting a lot of heat with dude's position. Before we kill him, though, a truth gonna be told about his style, fucking fraud-ass nigga. You with it, dawg? Fuck you gots to lose? You already a cop-killer. You all hood in my book—Pimping." He laughed and sipped the suds from the bottom of the golden can of malt liquor.

Chapter Nineteen

Sade

My lawyer's friend attorney, Steve General, shook my hand. "How are you doing?"

He had curly grey hair and thick-rimmed glasses. His brown tweed sports jacket clashed violently with his red polka dot bowtie. He smiled as he sat on the other side of the table. "I'll call you if I need you," he told the two guards.

The officer cuffed my hand to a ring on the bolted down table and tugged at it to be sure it was securely locked. "Is all of that necessary, officer?" He looked at the officer.

"I can call down the warden if you'd like, sir," the officer said.

"No, no, it's all right," he said, touching my hand.

They left the room, and Steve pulled out a folder from his Louis Vuitton briefcase. He took a deep breath and showed me pictures of my mother's body in the house. I looked down at them and couldn't even conjure up a fallacious gasp of shock.

"You don't seem the least bit surprised. You have to tell me what happened," he said, folding his hands on the table.

"I haven't seen my mother in three years. Why would I be surprised? She lived with an asshole boyfriend. Why nobody bothering him?"

"He's missing. Listen, besides your bus ticket, they have nothing on you. They're just bluffing to see what you know. Now whether you did it or not is entirely between you and your God. In the meantime, I'm your defense lawyer, and I'm here to defend you, for the better or the worse. Can I ask you a question—If you weren't at your mother's house, then what were you doing down here on the day in question?"

I shifted uncomfortably in my seat. "How is that defending me when you're questioning me?"

"This is my job. Secondly, I'm not accusing you nor judging, but you do need to know that these are the questions they will be asking when you stand trial. You need to know this, Sade."

"Has my boyfriend tried contacting anyone yet? I need to get a message to him."

"I'll see what I can do. In the meantime you need to contemplate a bit more of what you might want to divulge to me next Tuesday."

"His name is Mack Eric. Donald will know how to reach him."

"Okay, Sade." Steve lifted his briefcase. "Look, don't you worry. Everything's going to be all right." He smiled and shook my hand. He tapped on the door, and the guard opened it.

Then the guard and another officer escorted me back to my cell, where I jumped up on the top bunk and placed my hands behind my head. I stared up at the ceiling at the decrepit spots and peeling paint. I tried imagining the spots coming together to form me and Mack kissing.

Then it turned into him kissing some other bitch behind my back that was in the shape of old pink bubblegum. *He ain't tried looking for me. It's been a week, and I know he out there fucking them hoes. I just know it.*

Chapter Twenty

Mack

Joi screamed as I tickled her clit with my tongue then sucked it between my lips. "Oh my God, Mack, please . . ."

I quickly moved my lips back and forth, sensually molesting her hot air balloon with pinpoint accuracy, awaiting for her to bust.

She grabbed my head, wildly clawing at my neck like some vicious tiger hungry for meat, and opened her trap wider.

I crawled further into the middle of the liquefied cotton candy, her walls collapsing around me and drenching me from head to shoulder with some of nature's finest shampoo. A woman's sweet nectar.

We both got up on our knees, and she wiped her wetness off my chest and licked it off her fingers. She reached for my dick with the wet hand and placed her fingers in my mouth with the other. I nibbled on each one and licked in between her fingers.

Then she pulled my hand down into her bushy forest and circulated it around her flapping wings. She then cocooned it inside her warmness and kissed me. Then she pulled me back and lay down with her legs wide open, her hands behind my back.

Then she said, "Fuck me."

Without hesitation, I pushed my way through her insides, and she yelled out. The porcelain lamps sitting on the nightstands shook as the bed's headboard bullied the wall with a constant, rhythmic banging. A picture of me and Sade dropped from the wall onto the floor and shattered the glass within the frame.

"Hold up. Let me get that," I said, diverting my attention over to where it fell.

"Uh-uh." Joi turned my head back to her. "You're gonna pay attention to this pussy, boy."

And I did just that, violating our home, her side of the bed, and most of all her trust in me. I felt an instant connection toward Joi ever since the first day I laid eyes on her. With each drop of perspiration that dripped off my forehead and into Joi's mouth I started to realize that my feelings for Sade were beginning to drift. Our mouths were wrapped around each other's so tightly, I could actually feel her resuscitating life back into my sexual drive.

Chapter Twenty-one

Sade

I could almost feel Mack fucking. All I could do was cry in my top bunk. I had that money now and was going to pull him up out of that bullshit life he was in, but some niggaz just don't know a good thing when they got it.

The fucked up part of it all was, here I was facing a murder charge, and all I could think about was him. When a man has your mind so warped that you lose conception of all space and time, that's when you know your ride has been officially pimped.

Chapter Twenty-two

Mack

When I finally found out where Sade was, she was standing trial in a Virginia courtroom. It was my first time seeing her since she had left. She sat before the judge next to some local defense lawyer. Her lawyer, who she had never referred to, and I, along with Anton and Joi, sat on the second row of benches away from her. Three weeks of confinement did her a major disservice. She had a bruise under her left eye, and her hair looked like as if it ran off a road into a precipice. Her lips were chapped, and her spirit had been deflated from the head-on collision with fate. And the judge had a solid history of sentencing killers to death row.

Sade looked back and smiled at me and Ton, until she saw how closely me and Joi was sitting beside each other. She stood up and blurted out, "Who the fuck that bitch?"

Her lawyer quickly grabbed her by the wrist and pulled her back down, but she continued turning her head toward us, tears rolling down her cheeks. Unable to control her anger, she whipped her head around once more as the judge went through her case file.

"She's why you ain't been looking for me? You trifling-ass nigga."

Joi squeezed my hand tightly and quickly raised both our hands up toward the ceiling with a smile.

At the end of the day, y'all, I knew where she'd been all this time. I had called the two Ds who extradited her. I just felt as if she was beginning to crowd my space and trying to stagnate my hustle.

Never in a million years did I think she was coming down to kill her mother. I wasn't going to leave her here, but I needed time to get my shit up. I couldn't do it with her all up in my ass every day, bitching about this, that, and the third.

There was no way she was getting out of this. Her fingerprints were all over the house. But what really sealed the deal was when a surprise witness was brought in to testify.

When Glen walked through the double doors of the courtroom and took the stand, Sade shot up from her seat enraged. After he explained his side of the story, it became quite clear that Sade's intentions were malicious, heartless, greedy, and murderously heinous, beyond a shadow of a doubt. And that very shadow would forever shroud her days of a lifetime sentence without the possibility of parole. She was charged with attempted murder upon Glen. And Glen was handed ten years for being an accessory to the murder, with the possibility of parole in two years for good behavior.

I watched that bastard smile and wink at Sade, whose reaction to her sentence was silent and unemotional when the judge's gavel slammed down and solidified it.

"I'ma get you out, baby," I promised her.

As she was escorted out of the courtroom, she whispered, "Don't leave me here."

Joi commented, "She looking kinda trifling."

Glen was surrounded by officers as they secured his hands and ankle bracelets.

We stared at each other with uncertain familiarity. He stared at Joi the same way. He smiled again as he walked past us three then stopped.

"You the boy from New York, huh?" he said, still smiling as the officers shoved him along.

"What you gonna do, man?" Ton asked.

I wasn't going to be able to see her until the next morning during visiting hours. "This is some fucked-up shit. I don't know what I'm going to do, man. I need to go and see her before we leave."

We sat at the table across from one another in complete silence for the first five minutes of my visit.

"You played me, Mack. I don't even know what to say or think." She rubbed her eyes swollen from lack of sleep.

"What you talking, Sade? I didn't even know where you was at."

"Could it may be because you was sticking your dick where it got no business being stuck? The bitch all out there holding your hand up like y'all just won a relay race or some shit."

"It's not even like that, babe. She's the work I was telling you about. It's not just for me, it's for us."

"Bullshit, Mack. I've been down here for three weeks, and you left me here to fuck another bitch, then have the audacity bring her here with you?"

"There should be other shit on your mind besides who I'm fucking in bed at night, Sade. You up in here facing life. Get your mind right. How'd you ever get yourself in this shit anyway? Killing your own mother? When I spoke to you on the phone you said she was all right. Everything was all right. You know you could've told me. I would've came right down here and scooped you. Why'd you do it?" I softly asked, looking around.

She angrily replied, "She didn't love me."

"So what? A lot of parents don't love they kids. Yo, you was out in New York doing just fine with me. Why you come down here and spaz? Now shit is all fucked-up, baby. I'm going to speak with my lawyer, not to be confused with the lawyer you had on retainer that I never knew of. What's up with that?"

"Look, Mack, what's done is done. I'm just sorry I didn't make sure that asshole was dead when I shot him."

"So, with all that being said, how in the fuck do you think I can get you out of this?"

"You better think of something. Come here," she said, closely borrowing my ear, "I have some money put away that I want you to use to get me a new attorney. I'm not trying to do life. Fuck that!"

She whispered into my ear again, and my eyes widened when she told me the amount.

A female C.O. straightened out her holster. "That's too close."

"That's right. I got the money," she boasted. She quietly told me a sequence of numbers to access the dummy account. "You got it?" She looked around.

"Yep. 4–8–8–7–4–2, right?" I really couldn't be mad about her not telling me about her hidden agenda. I still had money to get from Stan's safe in Mount Vernon.

"Please get me out of here. The money will help get me proper defense for my appeal."

"All right." I stood up.

"So is that the bitch working for y'all?"

"Who? Joi? Yeah, that's her. I promise you, ma, that it's just strictly business."

"I hope so because I had a bad dream that you was fucking someone else." Sade leaned back into her seat.

"No," I quickly said, "never that. We're going to get you out of here. Well, at the most, a reduced sentence. Trust me, I'm on the job."

She stood up, and we hugged. She held on and securely pressed her lips against my cheek. "I love you, Mack. You're all I have."

"That's too close," the female officer said.

Chapter Twenty-three

Mack

It'd been a week since I'd last seen Sade, and a month further into the bond developing between me and Joi, which had reached to the point where I moved her out that apartment and in with me. She was a true go-getter and was strictly about the paper. Me, her, and Ton drove out to Mount Vernon to a small yellow house in a development for the elderly. *This would be easy*, I thought, *in-and-out type shit*. I told Ton to keep the car running while I hid behind the bushes.

Joi, dressed like she was a real estate agent, knocked on the door for directions.

"Who?" the frail voice responded, clicking and clacking the lock before finally opening the door. Her hair was white and wrapped in a bun, and the cane supporting her light weight shook in her tiny hand.

As close as I was standing by the door, she never even sensed I was to her immediate left behind her bushes. I wanted to be sure she was alone before just running up in there.

"Hi. I'm Shirley from Century 21. Listen, my car broke down over there," Joi said. "I'm waiting for the tow truck now."

"Well, come on in, Shirley," Stan's grandmother offered. "I don't get much company 'round here no more since my grandson passed. He was playing basketball right across the street over there." She pointed to the driveway of the two-car garage. "He was playing basketball with some friends when a car just zoomed down the block and started shooting." She shook her head.

I whispered, "Psst," to Joi.

She waved me off with her hand and slowly smiled her way inside the house, leaving the door partially cracked.

I looked around then quickly darted inside. The old lady startled easily as she spun around and lost her balance, falling on her shoulder. "Oh, Lord, it hurts," she said crying.

"Shut the fuck up, bitch, and tell us where the money at," I said, bending by her side.

Suddenly her mouth opened wide, along with her eyes, and a foamy pool of saliva began to develop at the back of her throat. She gripped onto my arm and squeezed.

I jerked my arm away. "What's wrong with her?"

"I think she having a stroke."

"We don't have the time for this. Give me the key," I said, holding out my hand for it, "and you stay here with her."

"Uh-uh, I'm not standing here while she dying."

"Then come on. Where he keep the shit?"

By the time we finished cleaning out his safe, the old lady was as dead as the beef between Biggie and Pac.

I stepped over her corpse. "God bless the dead and shit."

"Sorry, granny. We all gotta go sometime," Joi said, lugging a heavy black plastic bag full of money.

I sent Anton in to get the last load, and it was a done deal.

We celebrated over White Castle burgers and a bottle of E&J.

The next morning Joi and me both was trying to conquer the consequences of a morning hangover.

"We came off, boo," Joi said standing up naked. "Oh God, my fucking head is banging."

The contour of Joi's back was designed like the road to happiness. It traveled up from the deep, dark depths of the narrow crack in her ass and, like an overheated tongue during intimate passion, softly raced its way up her back. It stopped at the nape of her neck and kissed it with a small, dark beauty mark. A tribal tattoo danced around her waistline.

She wiggled her hips a bit as she slipped out of her pink silk panties. "I'm going to take a shower." Then she reached in the drawer for a fresh change of panties and bra.

"Hold up, baby. Where we going to hide all that money? Can't put it in the bank."

"We'll think of something. Right now, though, we about to live like stars."

I guess I never saw all them dollar signs in her eyes because she always had them damn shades on, but I liked that.

"No, we can't do that. We can't just up and start buying shit out of nowhere. Niggaz is still out there on the street trying to find out who killed Stan. Now how you think it's going to look when I just start pulling a flashy move out of nowhere? What you think Coke going to think?"

"Come on, are you serious? I thought you was the man, Mack. Ain't that what you told me? 'I got your back. I'm in control.' Was you fronting?" She pulled a tee shirt over her bare chest. "Is that what it was? You was just acting?"

"I don't front."

"So don't be acting like you can't run the show," she said and walked into the bathroom.

Chapter Twenty-four

Anton

"So here's where we at," Cocaine said to me as we sat on a couch in his basement. "I want to know what's going on." "What you talking about now, Coke? I'm off the streets. I'm in the house every day. What I do wrong now?"

"I was going through the numbers on the houses and keep coming up short. Know anything about that? I mean, you and my brother is the only ones in charge of collections, so tell me something good."

"Naw, naw, man"—I held my hands up—"you not putting that shit on me. I ain't never shorted you or stole shit."

"Who said anything about stealing? I didn't. So if you not taking shit, then you saying it must be my brother?"

I thought for a moment then cracked a smile. "You fucking with me, ain't you?"

Gordy came walking out the back room with his gun out. "Nigga, you was shivering." Gordy laughed out loud along with Coke. "We was just fooling with you, nigga.

Just wanted to see if you was going to say anything you wasn't supposed to." Gordy slapped my shoulder.

"Yeah, you was acting like a little bitch for a second," Coke said.

"Y'all niggaz play too much." I sat on the couch. "I hope this the last time we gotta go through this, man. I'm good, I keep telling you."

"Yeah, this the last time. I just really needed to be sure."

"And are you really sure this time, man? Because I can't keep doing this shit here."

Cocaine lit a cigarette. "Why don't you ride with us to Phenomenon tonight?"

"Naw, I got shit to do, but I'll be through later on."

This time I was packing but was glad I didn't have to use it. I kill these pigs for OPT, and now they wanna kill me. *It's too late to back out now*, I thought as I rode the Southern State Parkway. The red dial of my speedometer pushed ninety-five mph, and the engine heated up and roared. Wind blew in my face and pushed my cheeks back, as I hit one hundred, with no pigs for miles around. I took to the sharp turns in the road like a safety pin on point. I flew under the overpass like a mid-life crisis then swerved into the middle lane. I pulled a Mary J. Blige on them and made love to the road without a limit. I bullied the gas pedal to the floor, and smoke started billowing up in back of my car. So I pulled over and let the pigs catch up with me. These boys was out they jurisdiction. I kept the car running. Six cruisers pulled behind me and beside me. Red and blue sirens painted the night sky's darkened canvas. Shit. I'm bugging, y'all, right? Here go the jakes on my ass, and I'm sitting up in this bitch talking about the canvas night sky.

The officer yelled through his horn, "Get out the car with your fucking hands up!"

The digital signs above the road read DELAYS AHEAD FOR THE NEXT SIX EXITS. I weighed my options as the first arresting officer stuck his hand in my car. I took off with his ass holding on like call waiting.

I pounded his hands with my fist. "Let go, man."

"Stop the car! Stop the car," he yelled.

"Let go before I take off on your ass."

I could see the back-up cruisers racing up to rescue they people in my rearview. "I warned you," I said, accelerating the shit out of my baby.

His arm slipped off the door soon as the dial hit sixty. The nigga dropped and rolled under my back tire. My back tire jumped up, almost causing me to wipe the fuck out. The other cruisers all skidded and swerved around son's body.

One cruiser with two officers continued the chase. And as if shit couldn't get any worse, traffic was beginning to pile up, and the goddamn "whirly bird" was on my ass too, shining the Jesus light on my ass. I'm literally thinking, *All this for me*?

Cruisers raced down from the opposite side of traffic, and the others closed in on me from behind. Two *D* cars from Queens happened to be passing by and joined the party, guns drawn and everything. I knew I was fucked, so I got out and lay face down with my legs crossed and my hands behind my back. I don't know, man. Next thing I hear was all these feet coming at me. I was drug, swung, zapped, beat, kicked, punched, flung, tossed, had the plunger in my ass, and then read my rights.

The two detectives walked over to your badly beaten brother and laughed.

"Ay, how ya doing? Detective Bobby Malone." He shook hands with one of the officers. "This here's my partner Jeff Cunningham. We was just passing along and thought you guys might need some assistance."

"What are you guys, New York?" The sergeant laughed with another officer.

"Yeah, so what of it?" he said, looking at me.

As I looked up at him, he looked at me a little closer. Then he smiled and turned to his partner. "No fucking way," he said, pacing back and forth. "First, I hit the lotto last night, and now this fucking piece of shit falls right in my lap. Well, I'll be a son-of-a-bitch." He lifted up my chin. "Anybody know who this is? Don't even guess. I'm going to tell you. This is cop-killer, OPT dawg, Anton Mitchell. What it do, homeboy?" He laughed, taking playful shots at my mid-section.

Bobby came walking back from his squad car with a print out photo of me.

"Well, I'll be damned. How in the fuck did you avoid us for so long? You're going to get the noodle for killing those two young cops."

"Make that three," said the sergeant. "I just got word the officer he ran over just died on the way to the hospital."

Jeff turned toward the lake past the guard railing off the side of the road. "Where's your homies now?"

"I don't got no homies."

"That's right, muthafucka." Jeff grabbed my shirt collar. "You *don't* got no homeboys."

Chapter Twenty-five

Mack

"You see the news, nigga?" Cocaine yelled through the office phone at Phenomenon.

"Naw, I'm watching the floor right now. Why? What's good?"

"This muthafucking Anton done got himself arrested for running over a pig. I thought I told you to off him a while ago. Now I gotta worry about his ass leaking. If anything come out of this, I'm holding you responsible, you hear that? You." He slammed the phone down in my ear.

Gordy entered the office drinking a can of beer.

"Hit that remote to the TV," I told him. "Your brother tell you about Ton?"

"Naw, man. What about him?"

"He got popped on the Southern State Parkway."

The picture on the screen displayed an aerial view of the parkway backed up with traffic and a white sheet covering the dead pig's body. The camera switched to a ground view of the parkway, and some white bitch with long brown hair looking down at her microphone then into the camera, a spotlight on top of the camera shining on her face.

"Good evening. I'm Angela Pileggi of Channel Zero news. As you can see in back of me there's been a terrible tragedy. Earlier this evening a high-speed chase between officers and an alleged cop-killer ended in the death of a young rookie officer when the perp's back tire rolled over the officer, crushing his rib cage. Anton Mitchell of Laurelton, Queens, is the man we mentioned to you a few months back caught on a surveillance camera at the local bodega shooting two auxiliary officers. Now he's being charged with the murder of three officers. We have no further information on what other charges may still be pending, but there is sure to be a lot more. This is Angela Pileggi of Channel Zero news reporting live from the Southern State Parkway on Suffolk, Long Island. Back to you, Ron."

"You think we should shut shit down for tonight?" Gordy asked. "Shut shit down for what?

The girls is working hard. Let them make they money. Ton ain't no snitch."

"You better be right because my brother told you to off him a minute ago. Now look. You don't think that nigga will turn R&B on us?"

"What?"

"He's gonna sing to them, Mack. Wait and see."

"Naw, he a rider. He'll just do the time and eat that."

"That's what you really believe, huh? Ain't nobody your man when he facing life and got the option to own a get-out-of-jail-free card. Come on, monk, you not naive."

"Yeah, I'm not, but I'll tell you this—I'd put my life in his hands before yours."

"We'll see about that." Gordy stormed out of the office.

I fell onto the black swivel chair and rocked back and forth, holding my head. *This nigga got bagged*, I thought to myself. *Sade's ass locked up. Who next? Me? Coke? Bitch-ass Gordy?*

The office phone rang again, and I quickly picked it up. "Phenomenon. Talk to me."

"I want you to shut shit down early," Coke said. "Send them bitches home, then come on by my crib soon as you done. We need to rap."

Immediately I thought of Anton's story, that shit that happened in the Bronx. But Coke wouldn't do that to me. We had history together, even though it didn't go back as far as him and Anton's.

Back at Coke's house, he quietly paced back and forth across his plush carpet. I'd never seen him like this before. This wasn't him.

He stopped pacing. "This shit really is fucking me up. I've worked too hard for what I got to let something like this break me. Stan's people is cutting all relations with everyone until they find who killed him. And they looking at everybody. I don't need this shit in my life right now. Fuck! I need to take a trip."

"All based on speculation of this nigga talking? You trippin', Coke."

"You always wanted to see what it's like to be in my place, so here's your chance."

"What you talking about, man?"

"I'm talking about you killing Stan. You think that wouldn't get back to me? And the bitch you got living with you is the missing bitch from the basement."

"Yeah, you right. I did it. He was competition for us."

"Nigga, you don't do shit unless I authorize it," he roared into my face. "You crazy or something, nigga? I run this shit here. You in my circle. You trying to get yourself boxed out." Coke was facing me nose to nose now.

"Get outta my face, Coke," I said calmly.

"Well, oh shit." He smirked and backed away. "Big Pimping got some heart now, huh? You think you bigger than me now because you bringing in some bitches? Do you," he yelled.

"Yo, what the fuck is you doing? Why you all up in my shit violating my space, baby?"

"Fuck it!" Coke wiped his nose. "I'm leaving for two weeks. I'm leaving you in charge of the bitches, all the houses, all the collections. See if you can hold it down. When I get back and shit's still correct, then you'll be that nigga . . . since you wanna be that nigga so bad. Shit."

"I can do that, yo. You see how much money we bring in on Fridays and Saturdays? I got it on smash."

"If I thought you didn't, you wouldn't be here. One more thing..."

"What's that?" I asked, biting a hangnail from my fingertip.

"Keep an eye on Cakes. I don't want her working while I'm away. I don't want her around none of the fellas. And keep that bitch away from the coke. You know the rules, Mack, right?"

"What's that?"

"None of the family is to touch her, you know what I mean. This includes yourself. You let her and that bitch you moved on up in there stay together."

"I got you, man."

"What's going on with your lady?"

"It don't look good. If a good lawyer can't get her a reduced sentence, she'll be spending the rest of her life in prison."

"That's real fucked-up. But look on the bright side—you got a much better-looking bitch at home now that listens."

"Yeah, I hear you, man. So I'm about to shoot on out of here. I'll collect the money from the houses tonight and bring it to you later."

"Sounds like a plan."

"So, you know where you going?"

"You don't need to worry about that."

Chapter Twenty-six

Sade

As I lathered the soap up in between my breasts while showering, I thought to myself, *Mack left me down here to rot in a cell for the rest of my life*. The suds ran down my legs and surrounded my toes. Two other women down from me kept staring real hard. I closed my eyes and zoned them out. I let the water run down my face then watched as it quickly washed down the drain, just like me and Mack's relationship.

After showering I was escorted back to my cell to change back into my prison garb. This CO who had been watching me for weeks and bringing me food, loved seeing me fresh out of the shower. I always dressed and undressed with my back turned to her.

I had a meeting today with the warden. Actually the warden and them two *D*'s from New York. They had some more questions for me.

One woman chuckled, saying to the other as I walked past their cell, "Stupid bitch killed her momma."

The other woman stared at me. "I know. I heard about that."

"Somebody got a problem?" I rushed toward the bars, only to be jerked back by two officers.

We got to the warden's office and rang the bell. We was buzzed in, and I was seated before him, the two detectives from New York standing on either side of his desk.

The warden asked, "Ms. Watkins, do you know who these two men are?"

"Yep. They the bitch-asses who embarrassed me at work. Didn't let me wear no coat over my wrists or nothing."

"Yeah? Well, killers don't get an option," Jeff shot back. "We got some questions to ask you, and we come a long way. So cut the bullshit out and listen up."

Bobby cracked open a folder. "Ms. Watkins, we may be able to help you, if you help us."

"I already gave everything I have to give," I said, standing up. "If you're looking for me to confess to anything else, try coming on Sundays during cathedral."

"Yeah, yeah," Jeff said. "I know you don't want to spend the rest of your miserable life behind bars. Do you? Or is it true what they say? A monkey can't be tamed less it's caged. You get what I'm saying? We need something from you. It'll save some lives."

"I don't snitch."

"You don't snitch?" Jeff laughed. "How about snitching to save your life?"

I sat back down in the orange chair and straightened out my hair.

"Y'all ain't even said what y'all want."

"Don't be stupid," Jeff said. "You know good and fucking well we wouldn't be here—ugh, ugh—wouldn't—ugh, ugh . . ."

"Jeff," Bobby said, grabbing his shoulders. "Warden, can you get him a cup of water please." Bobby pulled up a blue chair beside me. "All right, Sade, no bullshit. We want Mack. Now I'm not going to sit here and shit you. There's no guarantee you'll survive in here for the rest of your life. Chances are you won't. What do you think Mack is doing with that money you put into that dummy account?"

I looked at him in shock and he shook his head like, "Yeah, bitch, we know." Matter of fact, that's what he said.

"He don't know. Even if he did, so what? It's my money."

"Sade, come on, you mean to tell me that it wouldn't bother you if your boyfriend was out there spending your money? The money you killed your own mother for? Or that right now he's with some other woman, sleeping in your house, your bed. She might even be wearing his boxers. But that's what a pimp does, right? Spend a ho's hard-earned money. What? You think I do this for fun? Mack is being watched. He's doing a lot of shit."

"I don't understand. What you want from me? I'm in here. He ain't wrote me or visited. How I'm supposed to know what's going on?"

"We need to know what Mack is doing so we can get to Cocaine. Only person close to him is Mack. Only person close to Mack is you."

"What am I supposed to do?"

"What if I told you I can get you out while you do your community this service. If it succeeds we have ways of getting off all charges. White power runs deep." He held up the devil's peace sign at the warden.

"I'd have to think about it. I don't be getting down like this."

"Look," Jeff said, sipping his water, "I'm sorry for blasting you earlier. That Mack muthafucka only gives a shit about himself. He don't give a shit's ass about you in here.

Don't get me wrong"—He chuckled in a chastising tone—"You deserve every little bit of fucking time they're giving you, but we really need that Cocaine fuck to slip up."

"So you want me to go back to Mack after I was to serve life and just all of sudden be free?"

"You do that and we won't seize that $600,000." He raised his orange eyebrows. "It'll be all yours when you're officially released."

"You're not telling me what I have to do. Matter of fact, give me some shit in writing. I'm not giving up nothing until I see some signatures and witnesses."

"All we need you to do is to testify in court that Cocaine gave Anton the order to kill those two officers. You can't say you don't know Cocaine because we have pictures of you and him leaving the Sheraton Hotel on February twelfth of last year. Bet Mack don't know about that."

"Y'all is dirty."

Jeff said, "You wanna stay here, or you wanna go home?"

"I wanna go home."

Chapter Twenty-seven

Anton

I didn't go out into the yard of Bingleton State Prison until two weeks into my bid. I was still awaiting trial. I felt like this, though—When you caught, you caught. I know I ain't getting off, so why go through all the bullshit? Send me off and let me do my time.

A CO released me from my cuffs when I got outside. Damn, it felt good to feel that sun hit my face. Shit, even seeing a family of geese flying overhead was like seeing long-lost friends. I saw my OPT niggaz down over by the benches. I cautiously walked by the Salvadoreans fucking with the weights, the Mexicans exercising on the handball court, and the small group of Asians boiling rice with a magnifying glass. My niggaz was listening to this ol' third-strike, Ving Rhames-looking muthafucka named Resurrection kick some knowledge. I gave all my people what-ups and joined the circle.

*My mind's in a fucked-up state and I ain't
even president*

*A jungle wit' gorillas is my residence We
be in here swinging from vines Nigga fuck a
watch We got nothing but time, nigga Switch
to Swatch Spit on this corrupt system. It's so
full of bitches So full of snitches Full-time killers cooking in the kitchen These kids today play
like Van Gogh, they just don't listen to catch a
predator His ass sitting on a stool talking about
he thought she was nineteen Knowing he just
picked her up from elementary school. Hue-
man racers, racing the race, of racist racists
Racially motivated by racial rants of the other
races We know George Bush hiding Osama in a
castle Telling Trip, yo, he cool and everything,
but I'll do 'em if I have ta Everybody wanna
have juice, and wanna know who got milk Tele-
vised, subliminally diverted, so you miss the
increase in your oil bill Who the fuck got oil?
Where's the commercial for that? Who got Ken-
nedy? For the back of his hair mat He must've
broken a penal code Fucking Marilyn Monroe
Was it the masons or the mob That sent him to
his god*

"Y'all don't hear me though." Resurrection
wiped sweat off his bald head. "What's good,
nigga?" he said to me.

"I'm good. What's happening? That was some real shit you was saying."

"That's what I do, tell the real. I'm here to resurrect the dead and bring them to the light."

"Yeah, I hear you, yo." I turned to my wolves.

There was twenty of us by the time we took over the benches. I was that nigga now. I murdered three police and now Cocaine would see I was still a real ill nigga. Now I could put the word out on the street to pop that nigga Mack. Slick muthafucka got my half of the money from Stan's house in Mount Vernon. I ain't heard shit from the bitch-ass. Him and that bitch is about to post up like they hood rich.

Maybe if I hadn't been plotting so hard I would have noticed that all these niggaz was surrounding me. And y'all know already what I was thinking? *Oh no, not again.*

"A'ight, nigga," I said to Rock, who was leading them.

"What you mean, a'ight?" he said, unbuttoning his shirt. "Cocaine said to tell your ass he loves you but you gotta go."

I took the first swing, then these niggaz took me to the playground. After five or six right crosses to my eye, all I could see was the COs and inmates cheering and laughing. I swung wildly at the air while the wolves took turns tearing me apart. I stood for as long as I could, but the combination of kicks, punches, and an ice pick to my left rib made me fall to the dust.

With that, warning shots exploded through the sky, and everybody dropped. Teargas grenades ceased the madness but choked me up and made my eyes burn. Then the COs charged through the smoke and snatched me up off the ground. They quickly dragged me through the dirt and gravel into the prison and left me bleeding on the floor with my hands cuffed behind my back.

"I should let you bleed to death," said a tall, white, dark-haired CO. "The cop you ran over . . . that was my wife's cousin." He spat down on me. He then took a cheap-shot kick at my already bruised and bleeding rib.

More officers ran in and pulled him back while he fought to get back at me. And the medics ran in behind them and rushed me safely to the hospital.

It was two days later when I opened my eyes. Two shadows stood on both sides of my bed. As my blurry vision began to clear, the shadows became faces with badges. Jeff and Bobby.

"Hey, what's up, killa." Jeff pulled back my blanket to look at my wound. "Holy shit. Looks like somebody wants you dead, dawg. Three guesses who it is," he teased, leaving the blanket by my feet.

"I already know who it is." I reached for the blanket in pain.

"So what you going to do, dawg?" Jeff said.

"Fuck I'm supposed to do, huh?"

"Do what all the homies do when their back's up against the wall—Scream, boy, scream—because you is about to be one dead nigger up in here."

"Think about it, Anton," Bobby added, "you're never going to get a good night's sleep in here unless it's permanently. Something big is about to go down with Cocaine and we need to know everything you know about him."

"Hold up, man. Something big like what?"

"He has a big shipment coming in. Very big, that's all we can tell you."

"That's all you can tell me? But I'm supposed to tell you some shit. Fuck outta here. I'll take my chances right up in this bitch. I'm dead in here and on the streets anyway. You can't help me."

"You know, Anton, I thought you was a lot smarter than this. You don't even want to know what we're offering for your cooperation?" Bobby asked.

"I could give a shit less. I'm OPT all day. I don't say shit."

"What are you, some kind of fucking dummy, Anton?" Jeff yelled. "Cocaine tried to have you killed and you're still being loyal? Where's your main man Mack? He been here to see you yet? Any of your boys visit you yet? Nobody gives a shit about you, homie. Your own goddamned mother ain't even been up here to see you. Matter of fact, I spoke with her earlier this week. She told me she doesn't have a son anymore. Hate to be the bearer of bad news. That's some fucked-up shit, right, Bobby? No homies. No mother. We're the only ones who got your back, pal." Jeff pointed down in my face. "You really don't have a choice."

It took this for me to realize how stupid I'd been my entire life? Cuffed to a bed facing life in prison. Cocaine had taken me on a dirty ride down into the cesspool of regrettable consequences. And I gladly followed him as a child and still looked up to him in my fucking adulthood. The fucked-up shit about it is, here I was trying to prove my loyalty to this nigga by killing the boys, then he go and put the word out to have me killed.

"What you offering, man? Can you get me out of doing life?"

"You killed three officers. That's not going to happen. The most we can offer is maybe having you transferred to another state with a reduction in your sentence," Bobby said.

"A reduction like what?"

Jeff snapped, "Twenty-five years with no chance of parole."

"Naw. I want out and in the witness protection program."

"You must have something real big to tell us asking for all of that," Jeff said.

I looked over and out of the barred window. A slight breeze circulated throughout the room from the crack in the top corner of its broken glass.

"Come on, man, we don't have all day." Jeff pulled a yellow pad from his briefcase. "You sign your name right here on this line." He pointed at a line with an *X* next to it.

"What am I signing?"

"That you agree to cooperate with us totally and fully in exchange for a reduced sentence. If a conviction is made for two or more people and the shipment that's coming in proves to be accurate then you's just might be a free brother, instead of being here on the African chain gang." He laughed.

Chapter Twenty-eight

Mack

"I'm going to be gone longer than I thought I was," Cocaine began as he faced all the bitches and wolves. "I know a lot of you is going to have a problem with my selection in who I chose to be in charge. But, fuck it, this is my shit and what I say goes. Come on up here, Mack." He placed his hand on my shoulder as we stood in the basement of Phenomenon. "This the nigga right here. That's the way it's gonna be until I get back. Somebody got a problem with that, speak up now." He looked at them all. "That's what I thought. Now as you all know, that bitch-ass Ton is locked up. Who know what the fuck song he singing up in there? Probably, 'let's make a deal' or some shit. But I got word out up where he at. He ain't gonna be singing for much longer. It can happen to any one of you. We all took an oath to be forever down with each other. That means you shut the fuck up when you get arrested. When I get back, things is going to be different. There'll be enough money floating around to buy your retirement home early."

Gordy ran down the steps and whispered in Cocaine's ear.

"Shit," he said, pushing Gordy back. "Shit. That muthafucka. Where's he at now?"

"P.C."

"I don't care if one of them niggaz got to put a guard on the payroll. Somebody make that shit happen or we all go down. Go now," He roared to Gordy. "You see that simple-ass nigga," he said of Gordy, "I would never leave him in charge to run shit. He don't pay attention. All right, y'all, time to get to work. Mack, upstairs," he said, opening the back door of the basement that led to the upper office.

"What's up, man?" I said, sitting on the couch.

"Is you up for this, nigga? I don't wanna hear no bullshit when I get back. You see how it works. All you gotta do is collect the paper and send them bitches out on the stroll. If anybody get outta line," he said, reaching for his waist and pulling out a Beretta, "you put some of this in them." He cocked it.

"That a'ight. I got my own shit."

"No. This my signature right here. The streets gotta know that even when I'm not here I'm still here."

"Whatever," I said, taking it in hand. "So what's this big shipment? I mean, you ain't told me nothing about that."

"Mack, trust me, if this shit go down the way I'm planning it'll go down, we're going to come off. Then you, my nigga, will really be the nigga you always wanted to be. All the bitches you can fuck, all the street cred. Pimp-of-the-year type nigga. I'm ready to be up out this shit when the time is right. And it's about to be right time."

"I can handle it. I was born to do this shit." I patted the glass overlooking the floor.

"That's all I need to hear. I love you, Mack. You're my only son. Please, don't give our family a bad name."

"I'm going to make you proud."

We hugged like father and son, like an episode from whatever heartfelt honky movie you could think of. Shit, at the end of the day he was the only father-figure I had. I respected him and loved him as if he was part of me. He raised me mentally and taught me how to stop just fucking a bitch and to make money off her fucking other niggaz. Sade was my ho at one time, but I broke the hustler's rule and fell in love with her ass. She wasn't shit before I cleaned her up, got the bitch a regular job and everything. Then she want to go and kill her mother. Now where she at? Locked the fuck up. My moms used to get locked up a lot while out there selling her ass for that b-rock. Now where she at? Locked the fuck in a casket.

"I know you will, Pimping," he said, patting my back. "I'm about to breeze on down these steps here. The boys is having me a little going-away party in the VIP. You coming down?" he said, opening the door.

"Yeah, what the hell? I could use a drink."

I followed him, and we walked through the corridor's maze into a melodic collision featuring Frankie Beverly's joyful tales of "sunshine and rain."

"Yo, what's up, nigga this, and nigga that," spread throughout the dance floor and across the stage. Cocaine and me walked to the VIP. Champagne bottles stood firmly planted in buckets full of ice. Cakes stood up at the table holding a cake with a burning candle in it. She smiled as we approached along with several of the wolves. Cocaine pounded hands with the young thugs as I then stood in front of Cakes with a look of anger. Her smile reduced itself into a slightly, straightened, expression of questionable regret. He then smiled and kissed her as if she meant everything in the world to him. She kissed him back so passionately, it looked as if she'd forgiven him for all the fucked-up shit he'd done to her. For that brief moment it was just the two of them.

And I really love you You should know I want to make sure I'm right, girl

The crowd shouted over the music, "Before I let goooooooooooooooo . . ."

"Y'all hold onto your ladies now. We about to take it up a notch," the deejay shouted, while scratching the record.

We all sat and began popping them bottles. Glasses were filled, and purple marijuana smoke that momentarily subdued our souls left us sitting with our eyes wide shut. We cruised across the cloudy vanilla sky, and we all stared and laughed long and hard. I couldn't remember the last time I saw duke so happy. He was smiling, being affectionate with Cakes, in public no less, shit he told me to never, ever do.

"I wanna make a toast to my top employee," Cocaine said, standing up. "Stand on up here, girl." He pulled her up out the chair. "You been with me from day one. You always been a good bitch to me. You know that, right?" He lifted up her chin.

"Yes."

"I know I embarrass you sometimes in front of people, but I'm trying to help you. One day I'm not going to be here for you and you gonna have to know how to conduct yourself around other players. Or even if you just be out on your own, you gonna have to learn to always be a ho. You speak when spoken to and only talk when you're asked a question."

"I know, daddy," she said, kissing his cheek.

"I love you more than any bitch I ever known. That means a lot coming from me," he said, swaying back and forth from the bump of soda he'd just drank.

He really had me looking at him sideways all of a sudden. I mean, I know how he get when he loose and shit, but now he was just acting plain vulnerable, niggaz at the table looking at him and laughing like the shit don't mean nothing. I was going to change all that once his ass left. It was time for a younger, more official nigga to run shit. First thing I'd do is make Gordy my top dawg. Know why? Because he's just a dirty, black, heartless-ass nigga who don't care. He's reckless and will do anything for money.

"A'ight, boo. Let's sit. You're gonna fall," she said, pulling him down in the chair beside her.

Chapter Twenty-nine

Mack

"Big Pimping spending cheese," I sang on my way home in a brand-new black-and-silver Lexus truck.

Every week I had four to six more new girls wanting to work under me. Cocaine was going to be longer than the original two weeks expected. That gave me more time to continue making money outside of the family and more money for the family. I had chicks working for me that had absolutely nothing to do with Phenomenon or OPT. They was *my* hoes. Gordy handled all the initiations and doubled the girls' already expensive rate of one-fifty an hour to two an hour. Three hundred for two hours would get you everything the girl could offer—head, ass, and whatever fantasy she could to fulfill to enhance the missing excitement in the lives of these married or otherwise-involved men.

I really had to give Joi credit for finding most of the girls. For once, everyone was happy. Everybody was getting paid what they deserved. Even the pigs. Niggaz stopped bitching about me being in charge and wondering why I never had to do initiation. The first thing I had them do was put the word out to stop looking for Joi. She belonged to me. Naturally, it was assumed by this time in the street that I had been the one to murder Stan, but nobody made a move because they was paid to walk away. When they found out his grandmom's house had been robbed they was paid to turn their head. Life couldn't have been better. What took Cocaine almost twenty years to do, I did in six months.

I bought a new house in Elmhurst, Queens with a three-car garage and swimming pool in the backyard. I took Joi off the payroll and made her my better half. I bought her a red Excursion equipped with an expensive system that rocked the block like the crack epidemic in its prime.

When I pulled into the driveway Cakes and Joi was out cleaning their Vs. I beeped the horn as I pulled in.

"Yo," I answered looking down as the hands-free display screen blink.

"It's Gordy, man. I just spoke with my brother. He said to be on the lookout. The jakes is watching us."

"Long as this money keep rolling in, I don't give a shit if a nigga named Movado is watching us. We got paper, yo. Speak to whoever you gotta and pay them not to watch. Get it done, nigga." I disconnected the call. "What up, y'all. Daddy is in the building. Come give 'im some love," I said, getting out with open arms.

"Yeah, right," Cakes said. "You know better. Coke don't like nobody touching me."

"Okay." Joi rolled her eyes at me.

"I'm just fucking around. Where y'all fien'in' to go tonight, cars all looking shiny and shit? Somebody got a date." I smacked Joi's ass.

Cakes said, "What? We can't just look fresh 'cuz we some fly bitches? Why we gotta be going somewhere?"

"I know women. Only occasions y'all get all dressed up for is funerals, weddings, jump-offs, and after the jump-off." I laughed.

Cakes and Joi looked at each other and winked. They aimed their hoses at me.

"Y'all better stop playing." I backed away with my hands up. "I'm serious, y'all. This a expensive outfit," I said, pulling at the collar of my short-sleeve yellow linen shirt.

"What is that? Banana Republic?" Cakes laughed and let off a blast of water into my chest.

Joi's came next, soaking the crotch of my pants.

"See what y'all did," I yelled.

Cakes sprayed me again then Joi next. I ran around my truck, and Joi cut me off.

"A'ight, a'ight, I give up," I said with my hands up. "Y'all got it."

"You gonna take us out to eat tonight?" Joi asked.

"We got a freezer full of food, two women in the house that can cook. What we need to go out for? Go up on in that bitch and make me a liver burger." I laughed again.

Joi said to Cakes, "Oh, he think we playing with him."

"I think he do." Cakes raised the hose again.

"A'ight, we can go out to dinner, y'all. Just chill." I turned my back to make sure the door was locked on the truck and was shot with a quick blast of water to the back of my head. When I spun around, Joi and Cakes nonchalantly looked up and around and started whistling.

Chapter Thirty

Mack

The next day, while scrambling some green peppers, onions, and diced ham into a bowl of eggs, Cakes said, "Mack, Joi said to tell you she was going shopping then getting her hair done."

She was wearing a silk Japanese robe, her hair was wrapped in a bun and her deep cleavage was visible through the folds of the robe. I couldn't help but stare.

"What are you looking at?" She smiled and looked up at me while stirring.

"Yo, Cakes, man, I ain't trying to be disrespectful or nothing, ma, but you look good as shit. I don't know why you fucks with Coke."

She put the bowl down and placed it down on the counter. She put her hand around her hip and pulled the top part of her robe closed with the other hand.

"You ain't trying to be disrespectful? Nigga, I know you not sitting up here trying to cutthroat?"

"I'm just keeping it one hundred with you. Coke is old and played out. He had a good run, but the race is over, know what I'm saying? Coke ain't it no more."

"Ain't he supposed to be like your father role or some shit like that? And you just downing him behind his back. You ain't say that to his face when he was here."

"That's because I don't wanna have to hurt the nigga."

"Yeah? I think you bullshitting."

"Yeah?"

"Hell yeah, I think you are. You might have the rest of these muthafuckas fooled, but I know shit about you. So you just keep that in mind the next time you decide to come at me sideways."

"What you making with them eggs?" I said, totally ignoring her threat.

"What you want?" She released her grip around her robe and continued her stirring.

Just then Joi closed the front door and chuckled. "Yeah, what you want?"

Chapter Thirty-one

Sade

The prison bus ride back into New York City was a slow one. The bus was only moving at sixty-five miles per hour. It was 5:00 A.M., and the red sun was beginning to rise from behind dark green pastures. Only through the partially opened window with the steel mesh gate over it could I hear the roosters praising the social alarm clock that rang every morning at the same time.

It was crazy how on my way down here I didn't realize how very familiar all this scenery was to me. Now on my way back it was like I was leaving a piece of me down here with those forgotten memories. Wow. Even my old church. Chesapeake First Baptist. The first place I ever had sex outside of my older friend. I think Jehovah forever embedded that shit in my head as a memory of how messed up that was. I'm paying for it now.

I always wanted to be a dancer when I was a little girl. I wanted a better life. I wanted to be great at something, but nobody was there to push me. Nobody believed in me, nobody wanted me, but now somebody did. Yeah, the state penitentiary. I guess I finally got my wish.

As we exited the state of Virginia, I looked back at what would probably be my last visit. Tears freely flowed down my face as I put my head against the window's gate.

"Bye, Mom," I whispered.

Detective Jeff put me into the back seat of his car at the bus depot. He asked, "Long ride?"

"I slept."

"I gotta drive over to Thirty-fifth and East. Bobby over there waiting for me. You're not in a rush or anything, are ya?" He looked at me in the rearview mirror and laughed.

"Why you always got something slick to say?"

He looked back up into the mirror and kept driving. Bobby flagged us down on the corner of Thirty-second street, and Jeff leaned across the front seat and opened the passenger door.

Bobby stepped inside. "Sade, you made it. Glad to see you."

"I bet you are."

"What's that supposed to mean?"

"That I got something you want, or I wouldn't be here."

"You sure got that right, sister," Jeff said. "We got somebody you're going to be happy to see." Jeff smiled in the rearview and slowly nodded his head.

I sat in the interrogation room with Bobby, waiting for this so-called surprise. The door opened, and in walked Anton accompanied by Jeff.

He hugged me and kissed my cheek. "What's up, baby? I hear your man left you to rot in jail."

"That's not how it happened."

"Ain't what I heard. So you dealing with these silly muthafuckas too?"

"Don't got much choice. You?"

"That's enough of the *Good Times* reunion bullshit," Jeff said. "Sit down, Anton. You both know what both of you is here for, so somebody start talking. We took care of the hard part, getting you out here."

"Fuck it," Anton said. "Get my lawyer here and we got a deal."

"No time for lawyers. We need something on record right now or the deal's off."

Anton looked at me, and I, now wondering if any of this was a good idea at all, stared back at him. I didn't want to jeopardize Mack's freedom because of some shit I said. Then sitting here looking at this bitch, Anton, about to tell everything he knew about everybody was bananas. He quickly signed his name on the paper and began squealing.

"When, Anton? Where, Anton? Why, Anton?" were some of the questions posed to him by Detective Jeff.

"I can show you where three bodies is at right now. See, Coke got this—"

Jeff held up his hand. "Who the fuck is Coke?" he said, putting a tape recorder on pause.

"Cocaine."

"Then say his name. Go on."

"He got this Beretta with these special hollow-tip bullets, right, and h—h—he got his initials put around the waist of each one. So, like when the bodies is found, niggaz know who made it happen."

I was plain disgusted with his ass. And even more so when he began mentioning Mack's name. He wasn't even asked about him.

"Then his right-hand man Mack . . . yeah, I hear he running the show now while Coke, I mean Cocaine, out of town on some business."

"Yeah, that muthafucka is going down real soon," Jeff said with fire in his eyes.

"Go on." Bobby sat on the edge of the desk.

"Mack killed Stan."

Bobby stood up and looked at Jeff. Then they both looked at me.

Jeff asked, "How do you know that?"

"Because I was there," Anton told him.

Jeff looked at me. "What about you, Sade? Were you there?"

"You can just send me back to jail. I ain't no bitch-ass snitch," I said, beaming Anton.

Bobby cuffed us both to rings bolted inside the table and opened the door for him and Jeff. "We'll be right back." He laughed. "Don't you two go anywhere now."

Soon as the door closed, I slapped Anton's face with my free hand. "I can't believe you," I said. "Mack's your friend."

"Mack ain't nobody's friend. Think he care about anybody? Not me. Not you. Not even Coke. He just skating along fooling everybody."

"I swear to God, you been a hater since day one."

"You think so? Hate on this then. Mack replaced your spot on the bed with another bitch. She's cute, young, thorough. You know how he like 'em. Why you think he ain't been to see you, huh? So you need to be thinking about that while you trying to protect him. He wouldn't do it for you. He's a user, Sade."

"Don't say that," I cried, my faith in him slowly slipping away.

"You know in your heart it's true, ma. He's a bitch, and I say we need to let that bitch-ass nigga and Cocaine fall. I know everything."

I turned to look in the mirror on the wall and realized it was a two-way mirror. I could've sworn I saw Detective Jeff point his gun at Anton then blow imaginary smoke from the tip of it.

Chapter Thirty-two

Mack

Me and Gordy had gathered all the girls together at the end of the night. One of them had been coming up short for the past couple of weeks. Even with the extra money these tricks was making there was a thief amongst us. We always told the girls to never come into work with their own money. This way we could account for everything that went on. By the end of the night no bitch was supposed to have any money on them 'less I gave it to them. And it was no wonder why Trisha, the girl Coke had to always yell at for being late, was doing a whole lot of fidgeting. It didn't matter if she was only twenty-four with five kids. If you want them li'l bastards fed, you have that ass to work on time.

I began talking to the girls, "You know, I thought once everybody started getting more paper y'all would be happy. I was wrong." I slowly walked past all eight girls. "I mean, tell me if I'm wrong somebody. Nobody can say nothing? That's because y'all all know who stealing. Tell ya what, though—there's a bunch of bitches just like you standing on line to be in your position, so if anybody want to still be working here in the next three seconds you better start pointing out the thief."

At first there was hesitation. Then almost simultaneously eight fingers all pointed to Trisha. One of the workers said, "Sorry, girl, but my kids gotta eat to. I need this job."

Some of the girls bowed their heads in shame, and the rest looked at her like, *Whatever*.

"Oh, that's some fucked-up shit, y'all. Y'all just going to dime me out like that," Trisha said in disbelief.

"The shit don't matter none. You stole. You know the rules."

Gordy locked the front door.

I walked around the living room for a while then faced her as she trembled. "Why you shaking?" I asked her.

Gordy walked over to her and snatched her purse off her shoulder. She fell off-balance as the strap snapped off the end. "That's mine," she said, regaining her composure.

"You're not going to need it," I said, looking into her eyes.

Gordy dumped out the contents of her purse and only came up with a gram of soda. He shook his head back and forth. "It's empty."

"Where's it at, Trish?" I asked.

"What are you talking about? The purse empty, dude."

"Take off your shirt and pants."

She stripped down to her bare minimums and stared at me as if she'd just proven a point. "See," she said, removing her bra and panties, "nothing." She rubbed her hand across her heart-shaped bush.

"Turn around and bend over," Gordy demanded.

"For what? I'm standing here naked. Mack, you see I ain't got shit." She reached down for her panties and bra.

"Trish, do what you was just told," I said.

"Naw. Y'all niggaz is crazy. I quit."

I snapped my fingers, and four of the other girls grabbed her up. Two grabbed her arms, while the other two grabbed hold of her legs.

I walked around to her back and gave Gordy the word. He caved in her stomach, and she forcibly bent over, revealing crisp hundred-dollar bills neatly folded up in the crack of her ass.

"I never thought I'd say this, but, sweetie, you is completely assed-out. Fuck her up right now, y'all, or you next," I told them.

Gordy cracked her jaw with an uppercut, and the girls made her wish she was rolling through the hood just to say, "What's up," but she wasn't. She was just rolling on the floor, trying to get her ass up. Every once in a while she'd catch wreck, but with two men in the house adding to the melee, all she could do was play like that Maybelline bitch and cover up.

As we parked in a White Castle parking lot in Hempstead, Long Island, Gordy bragged, "Did you see how that bitch crumbled when I snuffed her?" He kissed his fist. "That bitch dropped like a fly."

"She deserved it."

"Damn, man," Gordy said as he stepped out of my truck, "it's like fo' in the morning and look at all them young boys up in there, son."

"I just wasn't trying to do the drive-thru thang. We getting our food and bouncing. Five minutes."

"A'ight, man."

We entered the dirty little castle and waited in line. The late-teenage and twenty-something-year-old boys threw food back and forth across the table at each other and made as much noise as they could. We paid absolutely no attention to them, until a fish sandwich with extra tartar sauce sliding out its ends and meant for one of the boys running by Gordy hit his three-hundred-dollar denim outfit.

Everything got quiet.

Gordy slowly turned around and pulled the tartar off his sleeve.

I grabbed the bags from the counter. "A'ight, Gord, we got the food. Let's be out." I knew how Gordy was. If I'd given him a second longer to react, it wasn't gonna be pretty. You can always tell when niggaz is dumb, though, because you never know who be packing when you talk shit.

One of the assholes said, "Yeah, better keep walking, bitch!"

Gordy wasn't going to let that shit fly.

I dropped the bags and followed him as he rushed back inside.

He pulled out his gun. "A'ight, I'm not gonna even play the who-said-it game. I'm popping who I *think* said it."

When he cocked the jammie, they started arguing amongst each other about who said it, until the instigator was pushed to the front line.

Gordy smacked his face and made him strip. He cried as he took off his clothes. Nobody was laughing when Gordy made him run through traffic to the other side of the street. I made his friends lay on their stomachs, with my gun on them.

"I should shoot one of you clown-ass niggaz for tryin'a play me. I'm a grown man. Know who you fucking with—It's Gordy from Queens, niggaz." He let off a few shots in the air.

"Come on, man." I grabbed his arm. "We gotta go."

Gordy gave one of the boys a kick to the head before jumping in the ride with the dude's clothes from the castle. Then he yelled out to the boy across the street, "Get home to y'all's momma!"

When the restaurant was no longer in the rearview, Gordy threw his clothes out the window. He laughed out of control. "Now I ain't had that much fun in a long time."

"Fun, nigga? Intimidating kids is fun for you? Nigga, we both on video in the store, both of us, all because of you and your temper."

"Yo, what the fuck is wrong with you? You just gonna let some kids throw food at you and walk away? So one day when I'm walking down the street I see that same muthafucka and he thinking, *There go that bitch I threw a fish sandwich at, and he didn't say shit. Let's see what he'll do if I throw some bullets at him.* That's how these niggaz be thinking. I thought you was coming along, dude, but you really making me start to question your character again."

"Question my character? Ain't I been making shit happen? We all got more money, bigger houses. What else you want from me?"

"A real and official initiation."

"Fuck an initiation. I don't wanna hear no more shit about that. Me and your brother worked that out a long time ago."

He responded with a devious smirk, "Yeah, that's what I keep hearing."

Chapter Thirty-three

Mack

An early morning knock on my front door un-ravelled Joi's pretzel-like twist from around my neck. "Mmmwa," Joi said, pecking my lips. "You want me to get that?"

I sat up off to the side of the bed and planted my feet down into the root of my Christian Elijah sandals. "That probably ain't nobody but Gordy. I had to give his black ass a serious tongue-lashing last night."

"Yeah? What he done did now?"

"It's not important." I pulled up my boxers then walked to the front door.

"Mack," the voice called after tapping the door. "Eric Williams."

"Baby, who is it?" Joi yelled from the back. "Tell Gordy's black ass to come back later. We sleeping."

"Yeah. What's up?" I said through the peep-hole.

Detective Jeff tapped on the hole. "It's the muthafucking po-po, Mack."

"The fuck are you doing here, man?"

"We need to talk. Trust me, when I tell ya, it'll be beneficial to your health."

"I don't know what you're talking about, man. You got a warrant for my arrest or something? Because if you don't, then get your ass off my property."

"No problem," Jeff said. "Say, Mack, did you mean to shoot the phone inside Stan's house the night he was killed?"

I began unlatching the locks on the door and opened it. Joi walked out from the back wearing some sweats and a wife-beater on top of a black sports bra. Jeff and Bobby walked inside and stood by the door as I closed it. "Who's Stan?" I asked, playing dumb.

"Can you believe this guy?" Jeff said. "You let us in your house then ask who's Stan? I see you didn't waste any time finding a new girlfriend." He looked at Joi.

"You know how I do—One dead bee don't stop the hive from making honey."

"What the fuck kinda bullshit was that?" Jeff laughed. "You hear this guy, Bob. Well, look

here, Eric, I know some snazzy pimp talk too.
See if you can follow this—Your ass is grass," he
said with a straight face. "There are people coming all out the woodwork with your name smack
dab in the middle of trouble."

"I don't know what you're talking about. I just
help run a club out in Rockaway, that's it. All this
stuff about killing some cat named Stan is crazy.
I work every night. I'm legitimate."

"Let's cut to the chase," Bobby said, taking
over. "We spoke with Sade."

"Sade?"

"Yes, Sade. You do remember her, right?"

"Yeah, it does seem to ring a bell."

"Anyway, if you want to save your own ass, we
suggest you start talking. Can we sit?"

"No, y'all can't sit," Joi told him. "You got a
warrant? Do he got his lawyer present? I don't
think so. So how about y'all sit this one out on
the other side of the door." She opened the door.

"Do you really want us to leave?" Jeff asked
her.

"The door is open."

"I think you better reconsider," he said walking past her and stopping. "I don't think you're
ready for life in the big house. Joi"—He smiled
as her name escaped his lips—"Surprised I know
your name? Don't be. It comes with the job. Can
we come back in?"

"A'ight, talk," I said, holding Joi around her waist.

"Better get comfortable. This could take a while." Bobby sat on the couch.

After they left, I watched out the window until they drove off.

"They bluffing," Joi said. "If they knew something we'd both be in jail already."

"What if they do though? I hear Anton already bargaining for his freedom. And what you think he bargaining with? Stan's murder, and the old bitch in the house."

"You act like you did it or something. Relax, baby. It's going to be all right."

"Naw, I don't think shit's going to be a'ight. There's something shaky about them two dudes, especially that Detective Jeff."

"Something shaky? They're New York City detectives. All they got is hearsay, so fuck Sade, and fuck Anton too. It's all bullshit. I feel like spending some of our money today. I'ma wake Cakes up and we going shopping. If you're a good boy today, maybe I'll get you something nice."

As Joi stepped into the bathroom to shower, Cakes walked out the guest bedroom, her tight ass fitting snug in her custom jeans and her hips swinging with rhythm.

"You must've heard Joi talking," I said, scratching my balls. "She's going shopping."

"Damn, you are just too rude."

"What? I can't scratch my balls if they itch?

"You wouldn't have to, if you'd clean them." She looked back at the bathroom door, then at me. She stepped over to me, pushed her hand down my boxers, and tickled my testicles. "Is that better?" She kissed my bottom lip.

"What you doing?" I said, rebuking her advance.

"Why you always fronting on me? Everybody looking at me but you."

"You my man's wife . . . property—whatever the fuck y'all two got going."

"So you ditch one ho, move another in and make her wifey, then turn down some live-in pussy? You got a lot going on, playa."

"Cakes, man, I thought you had more class than that."

"More class than what? What class? You think it's classy earning my living by sleeping with niggaz I don't know?"

"Naw. I just always thought you carried yourself in a way where you wasn't ashamed of it, but you acting real crazy right now."

"So what now? You gonna tell your father on me? You gonna say, 'Cakes was throwing pussy at me, but I kept ducking'?"

"Shhh." I held my finger up to my lips. "I think the water stopped running," I said and fast-paced it to the bedroom.

I quietly closed the door. Joi walked in seconds later with a white towel wrapped around her naked body.

"Baby, I know it's kind of soon and you said to not make a big deal out of your birthday next Friday, but I want to do something real nice for you. Something I know you'll like. Is that cool?"

"Whatever, man. Just remember the boys is throwing me a party that night."

"I got you, daddy," she said, pulling off the towel.

She laid it out across the hardwood floor flat on her back, her Armor-All black titties glistening with droplets of water. Her freshly shaven jungle hair proudly presented her pink passage of pornography. Above her passage hung a lone beacon throbbing fervently with pulsating signals of S.O.S.

When I got down on my hands and knees and wrapped my lips around her Hershey's Kiss, which melted in my mouth like M&Ms under candlelight, and gave new life to her Milky Way, her stomach quivered, and she slowly turned her head from side to side, gripping both ends of the towel.

Chapter Thirty-four

Cocaine

After my short little vacation handling business, I went to pay my cousin Glen a visit in Virginia, where he was locked up for being an accessory to murder. I had some more business after that in Washington. I wasn't much for visiting niggaz in the joint, but he was family. I hadn't seen him in years. Not since he'd shacked up with some bitch with a kid. If he'd learned anything from me, it was make sure if you gonna settle down, always let it be with a fat bitch, or one with more than two kids. They'll take care of you when no one else will, because nobody wants the extra baggage.

"Look at you," I said to Glen from across the table.

"It's been a long time. I hope you brought something for my commissary?"

"No. How ya doing, Solomon? What's been going on, brother?" I said.

"You looking real expensive, cuz." He looked at my Rolex watch and matching chain.

"That's not important. Why you got me down here? What happened?"

"Well, I told you much as I could in the letter I sent. Did you read it?"

"Some of it. Bottom line is you locked up in here because you killed a bitch?"

"Not me. Her daughter did it."

"And you an accomplice? Man, you fucked up. If you think I can get you out of this, you wrong. I can't do shit for you."

"Look, man, I know we ain't seen each other in a long time, but I just need you to put some money away for me. I got two separate child support case warrants against me from God knows when. I done slept with every woman in Richmond, Chesapeake, Martinsville. I ain't got nobody looking out for me. You my only family."

"Niggaz really kill me." I laughed. "You talking like you want me to be sympathetic. I'ma leave you a little something in your account because you family. No more money after this."

"I love you, man," he said standing up to hug me.

"Relax, man." I pushed him away. "Relax. It's all good. You family, right?" I laughed.

"There's one more thing I need you to—"

"Come on, man, you using up your favors."

"The bitch that got me in here, she's on the women's side of this joint. I know you know a lot of people. You make shit happen. You always did. Even when we was growing up in South Carolina."

"So what you saying? You want me to get her done in?"

"Hell yeah. Her ass the reason for me being in here. There's a little something extra in it for you."

"Yeah? Like what?"

"Money. The bitch emptied out whatever her mother had left me."

"Where's it at?"

"That's the thing. I don't know, but I need somebody to find out."

"You know, Glen, I ain't seen you in years. What in the hell made you reach out to me? I don't know if I can fuck with you on that."

"Come on, man, it ain't like I'm asking you to do it for free."

"But, nigga, you is, 'cuz you don't know where the money is right now, home slice."

"Get somebody to shake her up. She'll talk."

"I know she will. That's why you in here now. What's her name, man?

"Sade Watkins."

"Who, nigga?"

"Sade."

"Describe her."

After he described her in full detail I just sat back and shook my head, not knowing whether to be shocked, surprised, or salty with Mack.

"What?" Glen rubbed his head.

"We got a serious problem."

"Oh yeah? What's that?"

"The girl you talking about, did she use to live in New York?"

"Uh-huh. With some nigga with a weird name—Fizzle . . . Fountain?" he guessed, trying to recollect what it was.

"Mack?" I asked, red-eyed.

"Yeah, yeah, that's right—Mack. How'd you know?"

"Because he works for me, and the bitch you talking about is his girl. Come to think about it, the nigga look a little something like you. Back when you had your shit together."

"So, you going to do it?"

"I have to talk to Mack first and see what he know about this money. The bitch ain't smart enough to hide something like that from him."

"She might not be smart but she crazy as a muthafucka."

"Crazy enough to start talking my business to certain people?"

"Crazy enough to bring down your whole shit. You better take care of it soon."

"And what about you?"

"What about me, Solomon?"

"Do I gotta worry about you talking to certain people, running your flap when it finally hits you what twenty-five years really is?"

"Man, if you thought that, then you wouldn't be here. Ain't that right?"

I sat there looking at him suspiciously.

"Solomon, ain't that right?"

I stood up and walked away.

He kept calling, "Solomon, ain't that right? Solomon . . ."

Chapter Thirty-five

Cocaine

"So let me get this right," I said to Craig, a very good connect of mine at an office in Washington, D.C., "twenty are ready to go, right, no questions asked because we went through this last year?"

"That is correct. You can do with them as you wish. We're looking at early as next month at the pier in the Hamptons, just as we discussed previously."

"What about the Coast Guard? I need you to be sure on this because if it fucks up then I lose everything. That's when I come looking for you with an army."

"Everything is in the process of being secured. There is nothing to worry about. Did you bring the last of the money?"

"It's out back in the van where you said to park it."

"Very well." He peeked out the office window. "By the way, you'll be needing the rest of these documents. Study them because there's crucial information there that you must know."

"All right, I'll be talking to ya."

"Have a safe trip back to New York."

"Yep."

"Yeah, Mack, this Coke. What's up, man? I ain't heard from ya. I hear things is going real good out there," I said to him as I stood on the twenty-fifth floor balcony of the Sheraton Hotel. The only lights on outside was the small blue and red blinking ones of the small airplanes off in the distance.

"Ay, man," he said over music in the background, "what's goody?"

"Apparently you, young blood. I'm hearing a lot of good things about you."

"You know me, man. Told you I'd hold it down."

"I knew you would. You are your father's son. It run in the family."

"I guess it does."

"How's Cakes? You been taking care of her?"

"I think she gained five pounds since you left."

"You're feeding her?"

"Hey, she gotta eat."

"Yeah." I chuckled. "I'm just fucking with ya. Say, Mack, how's Sade?"

"Haven't spoken to her. She cut off."

"Yeah? I hear that. Let me ask you something—Did you know anything about Sade and some money her mother left her?"

He tapped the phone. "Hello?"

"Mack, take the phone outside."

"Hello?" he said again.

The call disconnected, and I called it right back. His voice mail picked up before the phone could ring. I left a message with him. "Don't play games with me, boy. Call me right back."

That call never did come. And Gordy wasn't answering his phone either.

Now what the fuck is going on here? I redialed Mack's number.

"Yo," he finally answered. There was less background noise this time.

"Mack, what the hell going on? Y'all playing games?"

"Naw, man. It's mad hectic up in here right now. I ain't never saw it cracking up in here like this."

"My man, I was asking you something earlier about your woman. You didn't answer."

"Oh yeah. Naw, man, Sade ain't got no money. What you talking about?"

"I hear things, Mack, I got people all over, you know that. So you don't know nothing about that?"

"Naw, man. I don't know nothing about your people telling you Sade got money."

"Now I didn't ask you that. If you don't know nothing about that, then you don't know."

"Then I don't know."

"That's it then."

If it wasn't for this phone being a cell, I would've slammed it down on its receiver. Right in Mack's fucking ear. I wasn't feeling his attitude. He ain't never came at me funny. I'd been hearing he was acting a li'l powerful while I been away. I could hear it in his attitude. I hope that boy wasn't going to have to make me bust his ass and embarrass him in front of everybody.

The next morning I took a ride back down to the prison, on the women's side. I asked for Sade Watkins, and they said she'd been transferred to an undisclosed location. And I'm thinking, *Why would she need to be moved unless she was being protected*? Now, shit was beginning to bother me. It could've been nothing, absolutely nothing at all. But too much of this shit close to home was beginning to bother me. Out of a million muthafuckas in the world, how in the fuck did Mack end up with a bitch that lived down here with Glen when she was a kid? Then she marinates herself all up in my business and goes to prison for murder back where she grew up.

And the first thing they want to do is ask you, "What you know?"

Maybe I was just being paranoid and thinking too deep into shit. Why the hell would Virginia authorities care what a nigga do in New York? Yeah, I was trippin'.

Chapter Thirty-six

Mack

Me and Gordy was in the office of a small apartment building off Merrick Boulevard in Queens. We'd just leased it. Twenty-five apartments and all was occupied by our girls. You'd pay your fee inside the first office near the lobby then look in the photo album and pick the girl you wanted. There was one wolf standing guard on each of the four floors, ready to pop off if a nigga got unruly.

Every once in a while on a Saturday night there'd be one of them unruly cats that'd come in drunk off the Henny and try to get more than what he paid for. But there was hidden cameras and sound in every room.

We both saw a red light blink on the top corner of the monitor and heard Smooches screaming, "No!" Two dudes was in the room on top of her, having their way.

I chirped the guard, and there was no reply.

Me and Gordy ran up to the second floor toward apartment 2B. The guard was laid out on the floor, his jaw cracked. We stood with our backs against the wall on either side of the door, with our guns raised and positioned.

Gordy silently signaled to move on the count of three as her screams intensified.

We both rushed into the unlocked door and stopped before the bedroom. The two dudes was so caught up in raping Smooches, they never heard us come in. Smooches was being forced to suck one dude's dick, while the other violated her asshole with long, forceful strokes. She gagged, coughed, and cried as her hole was ripped at gunpoint.

Gordy yelled at the backdoor nigga, "Nigga, if you turn around, I'll shoot you right in the head. Drop the gun and kick it over here. Don't turn around."

The other dude immediately dropped his gun and kicked it over.

Smooches painfully crawled off the bed and began swinging on them both, and Gordy jumped in beside her, pistol-whipping both dudes. All the sorry in the world really couldn't help them, once the rest of the wolves ran up in the apartment, including the one they'd jumped at the door.

"You better come and get some of this, nigga." Gordy held up the nearly unconscious dude up by the back of his arms. "This nigga violated your shit. This your shit, nigga. He know who you is. What he just did is like breaking into your house and taking what he want. Fuck you gonna do about it? I know you ain't gonna let this halfway unconscious nigga make you look like pussy the pimp or pimp the pussy. Is ya?"

The other dude was knocked out cold on the floor, and everybody was waiting on me to make a move, a decision.

"Naw, these niggaz is a done deal. Get 'em outta here," I said.

As they was dragged out, Gordy walked past me in slow motion and mouthed something even slower, "Pussy the pimp."

It was bad enough that Gordy was hating on me, but now he was putting it out there that one of the girls got raped and I didn't do shit.

It got even worse when detectives Jeff and Bobby walked into Phenomenon late one Friday. They walked straight up to the office, and it wasn't hard to tell who they were. They walked in laughing as the door opened.

"Hey, great music," Jeff said snapping his fingers. "Who is that? Kool Moe Dee?"

"L.L. How can I help you fellas this evening?" I said, wiping down my desk.

"I heard that one of your bitches got raped the other night. Guess your name ain't as strong as you thought it'd be, huh? With Cocaine gone you ain't shit."

"Why the fuck is y'all bothering me? I don't know nothing about no rape, no bitch or nothing. That's my M.O.—I don't know shit."

"Keep not knowing shit," Jeff said. "Because when it goes down you're going to be the first one to fall."

"I told you all I know when you came to my crib. You're not listening to me."

"I don't wanna listen to what you gotta say unless it's information. You got a week to give me something. You get in contact with your pimp and tell him to call me. He'll know exactly what I'm talking about."

"That's enough, Jeff," Bobby said.

"Fuck that and fuck you, you little shit. You tell your muthafucking pimp we want our money or all this shit is over," he yelled.

"Jeff, I said that's enough."

"You know where I'm coming from, bro." Jeff poured himself a drink.

"Look, Coke is out of town on business, and I don't know when he'll be back. That's all I can tell you."

"Look, kid," Bobby said, "Cocaine made a deal with us and is trying to renege now. We've got way too much shit on his entire operation for him to try to dick us around. We're the reason why you haven't been raided yet. It's been a smooth operation, but your boy had to go and mess up a good thing. I don't like that. We don't like that. So this is how it's going to go from now on, unless you want to be in a cell next to his—You report to us once a week when Cocaine gets back into town. We'll back off some and keep a low profile. He's going down anyway, and we have two key witnesses that'll put him away for good."

"Man, Cocaine is my partner. How I'm gonna shit on him?"

"What you don't seem to understand, Eric, is that we have witness statements against you too, shit that'll surely bury your ass under the prison," Bobby said.

"I don't believe you."

Bobby turned to Jeff. "You want to tell him?"

Jeff smiled. "No, I'll let you do the honor."

"We have Anton and Sade holed up in a safe house in Connecticut. They're ready to spill the beans on you and Cocaine—Drugs, murder, conspiracy to commit murder, extortion, assault, the list just goes on and on, man. You're never going to see daylight again. You'll be locked in a super-max prison cell twenty-three hours a day, five minutes outside a day. And if by some strange occurrence you get a visit from the booty boys patrol, pretty as you are, it won't be nothing nice. You ready for all of that, Mack?"

I can't even front. They did put a li'l scare into me. I couldn't do no life sentence. But I couldn't snitch on my nigga. *Would he do the same for me*? This was the first time I'd ever asked myself that, and I didn't have an answer. "Naw, I don't think I am."

Bobby grinned. "I didn't think so."

Chapter Thirty-seven

Cocaine

My plane landed at JFK around 3:00 P.M. I didn't tell anybody I was back except for Gordy. Even though he was unreliable, he was dependable, if you know what I mean. He was right there waiting for me by the lobby when I walked out.

"Welcome home, man," he said, giving me a hug.

"What's up, boy? You looking smooth."

"Well, you know, Mack doing his thing. Shit, you been gone for a month and change. Mack done leased a building with his money and OPT money and everybody eating now."

I stepped inside his blue Denali. "He did what?"

"He ain't tell you? Ol' boy got a building, and shit is bubbling right now." Gordy pulled out and stopped behind a red Expedition truck.

"Nigga, you better be playing around."

"I'm not. You see, nigga," he said with a change in attitude, "told you he was a bitch."

"So you stood right there and watched him do that shit without me knowing?"

"I didn't know shit until he did it. And what the fuck? You the one who put your baby in charge, so don't be barking at me because your own dawg bit you in the ass."

"What you just say to me?" I turned down the music. "Say it again. I missed that."

Gordy knew. He never repeated what he said and soon began to move forward as traffic picked up.

"See, you can talk all that smart-ass shit you want to them li'l niggaz you be scaring. Don't think just because you my brother that the same rules don't apply to you. Now I been feeding your black ass, clothing you, putting money in your pocket, and if it wasn't for me, you wouldn't even know what pussy felt like. I brought you up, and you better start acting like you remember it."

"I'm not no kid no more, Solomon, feel me?" he said turning into the next lane in the road with one hand.

"So what that mean?"

"It means that we can pull over right now and see how much of a li'l kid you think I am."

"Do that then." I unfastened my seat belt as he pulled over on the side of the road.

Spectators rode by slowly while me and Gordy circled around each other, waiting to see who'd swing the first blow.

"I'm getting tired of you disrespecting me," he said, bumping my shoulder with his.

I unbuttoned my sky-blue linen shirt. "Stop being a crying bitch. I ain't taught you better than that, nigga?"

"You treat that nigga Mack better than you treat me. You don't talk to him sideways. You let him do anything he wants to do. I got my head beat in to join OPT. Why he get the special privilege of not getting his shit twisted back too?"

"Why you so worried about that?" I said, pushing him back.

"Because the shit is fucked-up. How you think everybody looking at a man?"

"How it look, Gordy? What you trying to say?"

"It makes it look like y'all got some special arrangement."

No sooner had the insinuation slip his mouth when I pushed it back down his throat with a straight right fist.

He stumbled back and swung a wild fist that cupped my jaw. We latched on to one another then rolled around in the grass, throwing blow for blow after blow.

I could see the impact of the punches above us in captions. *Pow*! *Zing*! *Kapow*!

"You give up?" I asked in mid-roll.

"You?" he responded out of breath.

"You're getting tired, all out of breath. Give up." I gripped around his neck.

"Fuck you. You give up first."

For just a minute it reminded me of when we was kids growing up in the foster care homes, happier times when it was just me and him against the world. But now we was living in a time where jealousy and hateful people made the world go 'round.

A line of cars backed up to watch the event live in the middle of rush-hour. I got up first and stuck my hand out to pull him up. He stared at me then smiled.

I hoisted him up. "Not bad for an old man, right?"

"Not at all." Gordy took another quick hit at my jaw.

"What the fuck you do that for?" I said, rubbing my chin.

"That's for the sucker punch from earlier." He limped back into the truck.

"You better come on. I can hear sirens." We hopped on the shoulder and got off two exits later.

"I don't want Mack to know I'm back home just yet. I want to see how he doing on his own. How Cakes?"

"I couldn't even begin to tell ya. Mack keeping her locked down like you told him to."

"That's all he better be doing."

Chapter Thirty-eight

Mack

"Yeah, let me get that ring right there," I said to the jeweler in the Upper East Side jewelry store in Manhattan. Me and Gordy was out copping some new ice for the wrist and neck.

The owner reached down under the counter and placed the expensive diamonds in front of us. The first chain she pulled off the tray was a seventeen-inch Rolex with a spinning diamond medallion with a red ruby in the middle.

"Come, you try on. This fit you well." The Jewish woman placed it around my neck.

"It's cool, but I'm looking for something a li'l more me," I said, pulling the chain off. "I need to have a trademark, something that says *pimp*." I looked in the mirror and winked at my reflection. "What else can you show me?"

"Oh, we have new item that just come in yesterday. I go get it for you. You wait." She disappeared into the back.

"You better get your shine," I said to Gordy. "We moving up."

"I'm going to get something, but this shit in here is garbage. These Jews be overpricing they shit. I wouldn't buy nothing from here."

The woman returned with a Gucci chain made of diamonds, platinum, and hints of twenty-four karat gold.

I bopped back and forth in a full-length mirror. "You can't tell me this shit ain't pimping, dude. Where the medallion for this?"

"I make for you by two week."

"You make for me in two week? How about one week? And I'll throw a li'l something in extra for you."

She took the chain back and weighed it then steamed it. She punched keys on the register then did some figures on paper. She slid the paper across the counter to me. "No good," she asked.

"Seven thousand? No problem," I said, pulling it out from my Louis Vuitton pouch. "Now about that medallion—"

The store bell rang when the door swung open and three masked men rushed inside with guns. "Nice chain, bitch," the tallest robber said. "Take it off." He put the gun right to my head.

"Please," the owner pleaded, "take whatever."

"Shut up," the fatter one of the bunch yelled to her. "Let's clean this bitch out," he said, passing through the gate in-between the counter.

The smallest one held Gordy at bay with a sawed-off shotgun. Gordy stood quiet but alert. I know he wanted to reach for his gun, but he'd never get to it in time.

The whole time along, the tall one kept his gun on me and looked into my eyes through his black ski mask. "Don't think I don't know you, nigga," he said to me. "You lucky I don't have orders to clap you, fake-ass, bitch-ass pimp. Should fucking shoot you just for the fuck of it, nigga." He pushed my head to the side with the gun.

"We gone," shouted the fat one. "We don't need everything. Let's get the fuck outta here."

The two started to run out but about-faced when they saw they man still standing in my face. We stared each other up and down, daring one another to look the other way.

He stuck the gun in my face. "I could kill you right now, nigga." He pushed it all the way to the back of my throat, and I gagged.

"Let's go, nigga," the short one yelled, and ran out with a sack of stolen jewelry.

He kissed my cheek and then slapped my ass. "We ain't forgot about Stan. Ay, yo, son," he said to

Gordy, "take your man home and get 'im cleaned up. I think the baby pissed his pants." He laughed and ran out facing us, keeping aim with his gun.

Gordy looked at me in disgust as I stood in a puddle of my own piss.

Joi asked me, "So you ready for your birthday party tonight, baby?"

"I'm ready for the party, not the birthday. I feel like I'm getting old."

"You crazy. You not getting old. Shit, you know how many niggaz out there wish they was twenty-nine and have what you have? A lot. You got cars, a house, street cred. And you got me. Now how you feel like you getting old with all of that? You're the man. You running the show."

"Sometimes it don't feel like that. Not when it feels like the niggaz that's supposed to be down with me is trying to set me up."

"So, baby, let's bounce then."

"Just like that?"

"Straight like that. We got the money to go anywhere we want."

"I can't just leave. Everybody's depending on me."

"Everybody like who? Coke? That nigga not worried about you. Why you the only one who don't see that?"

"I don't. I wouldn't have any of this if it wasn't for him. I can't bounce."

"And he wouldn't have what he got if it wasn't for the next man that put him on. You need to break loose from him before jealousy enters y'all lives."

"What you talking about jealousy?"

"You might think that it's all love right now, but when his spotlight shines completely on you, that's when you'll see a whole new performance. Ain't enough room for two stars on the stage."

"You don't know what you talking."

"But those detectives do. I love you. You saved my life, and I don't wanna see anything happen to you."

"Ain't nothing going to happen to me. I'ma always be good."

"I know you are. Well, you better start getting your clothes together tonight for your party."

"Yeah, you right. I still gots to get my truck detailed and get the tires changed." What up, Cakes? I said as she walked in the house.

"What's up, birthday boy?" she said, kissing my cheek. "What's good, ma?" she said to Joi.

"Hey, where you coming from?"

"I went to get those things you asked me about."

"Oh, no doubt. Take it in your room for me."

"What secrets you trying to hide?" I smiled and kissed Joi.

Cakes laughed. "Oh God. Would y'all two please save it for the bedroom. Y'all been acting so lovey-dovey lately, y'all starting to look like each other. I'm jealous. I'm the only bitch living up in here with no dick."

"Don't worry, bitch," Joi told her. "Your daddy'll be home soon."

Chapter Thirty-nine

Cocaine

Gordy was sitting on the edge of my couch at my other house in Jackson Heights, Queens, explaining to me the robbery he'd set up the other day. He said, "Yeah, Coke, the nigga pissed his pants and ev'ythang. He was scared to death, man. I'm starting to think this nigga ain't never killed nobody in his life. I wouldn't be surprised if the bitch did it. I'm telling you, Coke. Put 'im to the test. Give him an official initiation. We only taking him seriously on the strength of you."

"How many times I have to tell you to stop hating on the boy? Everything I do is for a reason."

"I hope so, man, because the last time you thought a nigga was real, you ended up putting out a hit on him."

"He handling the day-to-day, right?"

"I told you before he doing it."

"Then what's the problem? I don't wanna keep talking about this, Gordy."

"Ain't no problem."

A knock at the door broke the conversation. "Anybody know you here?" I said to Gordy.

"Naw, man," he answered, reaching for his gun.

I peeked out the blinds in the living room and saw nothing.

"Solomon Ivory, it's us. We know you're in there, so just open the fucking door," Jeff said.

"Put that thing away," I whispered to Gordy. I opened the door to see two smiling faces in front of me.

"Why do we have to start playing this game?" Jeff said entering.

"We had a deal," Bobby said. "Everything was going fine until you stopped paying."

"They're closing in on you, and without proper funding there might not be much we can do to help you."

"What you mean, closing in? We had an agreement."

"I told you a long time ago to slow down. We can't cover every angle, so now we have to cover our own asses." Jeff said to Gordy, "You got a staring problem or something?"

"Naw, man."

"Then you better stop staring like you want one."

"Solomon, it's like this. None of this would've ever happened if your boy Mack didn't have a girl that killed her mother. She talked about you and Mack, and the entire OPT organization, information we can use against you when the time is right. We have Anton. He's willing to testify in court that you ordered him to kill those two officers."

"Yeah, but you and I both know that you two paid me to have them killed."

"I see that memory of yours is still good for something. See if you can remember this," Jeff said. "We talked to Mack too. He wants to make a deal."

"See, I told you," Gordy blurted out, pointing at me.

"Shut up. What you mean, he's ready to make a deal?"

"Yeah," Bobby added. "We had a nice long talk with him and Joi."

"I don't believe you."

"We have two written statements from them both swearing that you have underage girls working for you after twelve in the morning. The two bodies he helped you bury in the woods upstate. The coke being sold in your bar. What I can't understand is why he doesn't know about the shipment?"

"Nobody knows."

"What else could it be but your namesake, smart guy?" Bobby adjusted his gun holster.

"Whatever you do in the dark will come to light, Solomon," Jeff said. "We had to find out through intel that you got a secret shipment coming in, and you don't let us know? What was you trying to do? Cut us out of our share?"

"How much is it going to cost me?"

"Cost you to do what?" Jeff asked.

"To divert attention from my package."

"Well, Solomon, the way I see it is, you lied to us, you tried to hide profit, and that's not right. We let you do what you wanted for years with no hassle. You get with this fucking Mack, who I've never liked, and everything turns upside down."

"So how much is it going to cost me?"

"Fifteen percent increase."

"That's not going to happen."

"You're trying to tell me how it's going to go? You don't tell me, I tell you, and I say fifteen, take it or leave it. No skin off my ass one way or the other."

"What I'm trying to say is I can only afford to do ten. Otherwise we don't have a deal."

After secretly congregating with his partner, Jeff said, "If you fuck us on this, I'll personally see to it that the system swallows the key to your cell."

Gordy couldn't wait until they left to say, "I told ya so," again and again. "What you think about your boy now?" he asked, a smirk of accomplishment on his face.

"Shut up. I need a minute to think."

"He been planning this, yo. The whole shit sound funny to me. I say buck that nigga and let's get back to how shit used to be."

"Naw, we not gonna kill him. Not yet anyway. Let him keep making that money for me right now. He think he the man, let him keep thinking that."

I was furious. I took that li'l nigga under my wing, and he just straight clipped the shit while I was in mid-flight. I knew those pigs was telling the truth because it was only shit me and that nigga knew. They probably told him he'd be top dawg if the information he gave led to my arrest, and like a dummy he went for the bait.

Chapter Forty

Mack

Anton had finally reached out to me by phone from an undisclosed destination while I was driving to pick up my custom-tailored suit. "Yo," I answered.

"Yo, what up, man? Did you miss me? I mean it's only been like four months."

"Ton?"

"Who else?"

"Why you calling me, man? You got a lot of people mad at you. Where you calling me from?"

"That don't matter. What do matter is that you got something of mine, and I want it."

"What, nigga? You fucking with them boys. I don't know what you talking about."

"You gonna know. You a foul-ass dude. I thought we was friends."

"I ain't nobody's friend. I'm a businessman who likes making his paper."

"That's fucked up too how you did Sade. But what goes around comes around. You gonna get yours."

"Think so? You dead anywhere you go, Ton. Coke want you dead, but I guess you already found that out."

"I'm still here."

"I don't even know why I'm talking to you."

"What it matter? You and that Joi bitch both been running your mouths anyway. The boys told me everything. We'll see who the dead man is real soon."

"Fuck you, nigga!" I ended the call. I said to myself out loud, "Nigga talking to me like I'm worried about something."

I changed into my suit at the store then drove straight to the bar. Gordy was just coming down the steps from the office when I walked in. He signaled me over to the VIP table.

"Birthday nigga," he shouted over the music. "Have a seat, nigga. This your night," he said, drinking Cristal straight from the bottle.

"You hear from your brother yet?" I asked.

"He'll be home Tuesday. I told him you doing your thang, making that money, that easy dollar."

"Yeah, well, you know me. Told your brother I could do it."

"No doubt. He got mad faith in you."

That wasn't Gordy's personality at all. Even though we'd learned to get along in the presence of Coke, it didn't change the fact that dude hated me. But I let it slide because we was about to party, and what could go wrong in that?

"Hey, birthday boy." A dancer began to grind her ass on my lap, her waist moving like liquid. "What can Lexus do to make your birthday even more special, daddy?" she asked, wrapping both her arms behind my neck.

I put my hands around her smooth, toned stomach. Her strawberry body spray persuaded me to lick it off her neck.

She pressed her neck against my lips. "You like that, daddy?"

"You taste good," I said.

Gordy poured me another drink. "Drink, nigga, drink," he said, putting the glass to my lips to guzzle. "Wind that nigga harder, Lexus. He ain't scared yet." Gordy slapped her ass. "Ay, the rest of y'all, get on over here. Y'all know the birthday boy in the building. Fuck the matter with y'all?"

A group of dancers walked over to me barefooted from the stage one by one, each one sexier than the next, their tits bouncing with each step of their sexually, aggressive strut. They surrounded me, and Lexus stood.

Gordy pushed the tall forty-two double D girl in front of me. "This the new girl."

"What's good, ma? You here to help me celebrate?" I said, sipping and smiling.

"Shut up, nigga." She stomped her foot. "Did I tell you that you could talk? Did . . . I . . . tell . . . you . . . to . . . talk?" she said, twisting her head as she spaced her words. "Lexus, this the birthday boy you was telling us about in the back?"

"Uh-huh, that's his ass."

"He don't look like much. You sure this the one?"

"Oh, that's him, all right."

"Hmm. Baby, my name is Storm." She rubbed her hands up and down the front of her thighs. "Get 'em girls," she said as Kellz directed their actions through the powerful stereo system in the bar.

Storm removed my blazer and unbuttoned my shirt down to the bottom. Lexus stood over her while she licked inside my navel from between Lexus's legs. Lexus put her tit in my mouth and guided it around my thick lips. The other girls softly ran their long custom-designed nails sensuously up, down, and across my neck.

Storm unbuttoned my pants and reached for the star. "Naw, fuck that. Take them shits off." She pushed Lexus to the side.

They both pulled my pants off one leg at a time until I was sitting in my boxers.

"Drink, nigga, drink." Gordy laughed and poured another shot of Jamaican rum down my throat.

Lexus pulled off her black leather snap-on thongs and tossed them to Gordy, who put them in his mouth and shook it back and forth like a rottweiler shaking the shit out of a chihuahua. She let her legs hang off the sides of my legs and grabbed onto my shoulders, sliding across my hardness and saturating my boxers with her excitement.

Meanwhile, the other girls standing on my sides gyrated their bodies in sync with the fluidly hypnotic panty-wetting experience.

Storm stuck her tongue in my mouth and grabbed Lexus's hand and stuck it down her panties. I tried to follow suit, but Storm pushed my hand away. "I'm running this show," she said, while Lexus continued to grind.

Lexus got up and ripped my boxers off from the slit in the middle. She put her soaking pussy on my bare dick and ran it in every direction, but in.

Storm brought back over the bottle and poured it out over Lexus's naked body. "Now clean her up, nigga," she said. "Lick it all off." She joined me as I licked alcohol from Lexus's chest.

Lexus stood up and back away. She popped her fingers in and out of herself, sighing deeply with her eyes closed. Storm stood behind her and assisted her in pleasuring herself, adding an extra set of fingers. Lexus wobbled at the knees and leaned back against Storm's chest, turning her head up to her. Then they began kissing, while the girls took turns stroking my shit.

Lexus stared at me and walked forward with a twist to it. She got on her knees in between my legs and blew hot air, causing my curly black hair to relax and straighten.

"Yeah, baby, go ahead," I said, closing my eyes.

"You getting all this, nigga?" Gordy asked one of the wolves getting the party on video. "Look at that nigga." He laughed. "Here, nigga, drink, drink." He handed me another shot.

Storm stood over Lexus and took hold of her hair while Lexus licked all in between my inner thighs.

Storm pulled her to her feet by her hair and reversed roles again. The girls all encircled me as Storm opened her mouth and hid my erection deep down in her throat.

Chronic smoke took the air hostage. Lexus dropped a bump of soda on her tongue and quickly ran over to me before it could dissolve. It tingled my tongue as she wrapped the tip of hers around mine.

The rest of the girls stepped out of their panties and began sliding their wetness across my bare arms after one of them removed my shirt. They shook their hips and clapped after every break beat in the song.

Gordy kept the drinks coming until everything began to spin. "Drink, nigga, drink."

The music began to speed up, and so did my heartbeat. I started to sweat, and it turned me on. I grabbed Storm's head and pushed it down further, while the girls clapped with each stroke.

While Storm gave me more head, Gordy took hold of the camera and pointed it directly at me. "Nigga, you ain't finished. Have another drink."

Chapter Forty-one

Gordy

I ain't got shit good to tell you about Mack. You already see it in front of you. All he really had going for him was a bitch, and Cocaine's name to protect him.

How long you think that can possibly last, living off the next man's name? My own brother starting to not come off as official to me no more. This nigga Mack doing what he wanna do, and my brother call himself watching him from the cut. Meanwhile, po-po all up in his ass. And this nigga still just like be easy, saying, "I'm watching him." What kinda shit is that? The *D*s you paying telling you this nigga snitching and you just like, *Fuck it*.

And these *D*s Coke paying . . . I ain't never knew that nigga to be dealing with the dicks and not tell me. And for the first time I was starting to look at him suspect too.

I wonder of any if the other wolves thought the same. Watching all this silly shit go down was really starting to make me wonder if Mack was holding something over Coke's head. And if he was, then why didn't he just off that nigga a minute ago? Naw, there was much more to this whole shit. Even right down to his visit with some long-lost cousin named Glen locked up for murder down in VA. Why the fuck was he connected to Mack through Sade, whose step-father just so happened to be our cousin? What in the fuck were the chances of that? Then the dicks started talking that snitching shit, and now we all looking at Mack.

Life was about to start getting real uncomfortable for his ass. He needed to be exposed, the fake-ass nigga. I had to find a way to see why my brother was showing this dude so much love. And you know what? I don't know why I didn't think of this before.

While my brother played hide-and-seek, I went over to his house one night. I had a spare key. I went down into the basement into a small office with a five-foot file cabinet. I unlocked it and looked up and down at the alphabetically ordered DVD cases holding individual initiations on each one of the wolves. From nine P.M., I watched one hundred initiations, hoping that

Mack's would be secretly hidden at the end of one.

"Damn," I said out loud, scrambling through areas of the room that could've been logical hiding places, "I know it's got to be here somewhere." *Why the fuck is he the only one with no DVD?* I thought, pacing back and forth.

I took a long shot in the dark and lifted the cabinet halfway up, and there it was, the initiation of Eric Williams aka Mack. I smiled at the DVD. "Look at this shit here, nigga."

This was going to be an event, so I went up and popped some microwave popcorn. I put the disc in and sat back. It wasn't what I expected, but it was what I always thought. You try to figure that one out, the rest of y'all, follow me.

"Coke," I said after dialing my brother's cell. "What's the matter?"

"Nigga, we need to talk."

"What you talking about now, Gordy?"

"I'm in your house."

"So? Just don't be fucking on my bed."

"That's not what I'm doing here, *mayne*," I said, almost in tears.

"What's the matter with you?"

I took a deep breath and moved the phone away from my mouth. I pushed eject on the DVD player and put the golden disc back in its special platinum-colored jacket.

"Gordy," he called, "answer me, nigga. What in the fuck is going on?"

"You wrong. Now I see what all this Mack shit about."

"You back with that again?"

"I found the disc under your file cabinet, the one with your boy's initiation."

I didn't go to check my brother that day or night and disregarded every call and message that nigga made and left. I finally had what I needed to expose that punk-ass Mack. But it wasn't going to be enough just to expose him. Killing him would be too easy. Some bitches and niggaz would miss him too much and forever cherish his memory. That ain't what I wanted. I wanted him to be totally stripped of his swagger. I wanted his ass to be straight embarrassed. So embarrassed, his own shadow would run and hide in the dark corner of a room. I wanted to see the nigga cry in front of everybody.

Chapter Forty-two

Mack

I walked into Luciano's pool hall out in Brooklyn like a fucking superstar, an entourage of wolves behind me. Images ahead and around me reflected off my dark shades and gave the fans a duplicate view of how I saw them through my eyes. And it was all love. It looked like they was moving in slow motion as I walked through the human aisle, being slapped on the back and kissed by every chick close enough to smell my arrogance. I was at the top and didn't have to climb no ladder to get here neither.

"We got Mack in the house," the deejay shouted over the microphone. "What up, what up?" I smiled, throwing my hand up at him.

I continued my *Hollyhood* shuffle over toward the nine pool tables all sitting across from one another, chain-linked lamps with bright fluorescent lights hanging over the color-carpeted canvases. Balls click-clacked off the surrounding walls of the table and rolled into designated corner pockets, like D.T.s rolling up on hustlas on the block.

"All give praise. Mack is here to stack some bundles. Hundred dollars a ball." I threw up a yellow-and-white four ball then caught it. "Come on, ballers, who wanna lose they money?"

Damn near the entire pool hall of patrons surrounded me, placing bets and sipping their drinks. Every move I made was clocked, reviewed, and tallied up as me being man of the year. Try more like a lifetime, though. I did this shit standing on my head all day long.

I smiled and looked around. "What's up? Who want it first?"

A blinged-out smart-ass said, "I want some." He stood with the stick between his hands, and planted on the floor before him. "Word, I'll take that bet." He pointed the stick at me and chewed his gum hard.

My wolves reacted quickly to the blatant disrespect, but I chilled them out. The li'l nigga had to be only about nineteen or twenty years old. More bets was placed, and the bitches' pussy temperatures raised a notch higher when I upped the stakes to five hundred a ball.

"So what?" the kid said, not ruffled by the financial threat. "Think you the only nigga wit' dough." He chalked his stick.

"Who the fuck is this clown, y'all?" I said, setting the table.

"You don't need to know me. You playing or talking?" He inspected the corners of the table to ensure it was level.

I struck the white ball with a long, smooth, stylish stroke of accuracy, sending all the other colors racing across the flat landscape. Some rolled and fell down in the pockets.

"Look at that there, son—three solids in already." I watched him as I eased around the table for a better angle on my next shot.

"Ain't that a bitch? That's on your first shot," he said, pretending he was impressed.

"Kids," I said bending over the table to shoot, "when you gonna learn not to fuck with grown men? You supposed to be looking up to me." I shot the three ball down the hole in front of him. "You know why? Because you fuck around and end up real hurt." I walked around to the other side of the table and chalked my stick again.

"You see, li'l nigga, I don't know who sent you. Or maybe you just built like that." I chuckled. "But you don't bet wit' niggaz you don't know because you never know what they'll do to you."

I tapped the scratch ball so hard, it jumped off the table.

"My fault," I said, chasing it down. "I gotta tell you, yo, it don't look like you gonna get your turn. Just a couple more balls and you can come up all that ice and shit because I already know you ain't got the paper on you."

Niggaz was on standby waiting to beat the soul out of son if he tried to dip without paying. But he wasn't by himself. He had some dudes standing off in the darkened cut while we stood out exposed in the still limelight of a Polaroid moment.

"It ain't nothing," he said. "We all gotta pay sometimes."

"You awfully calm for a nigga about to come out his pockets," I said, missing the last ball by an inch.

After that, the boy went on to hit every last one until it came down to two sticks and some balls. He shot and missed the eight and scratched the ball.

I turned and smiled at my peoples, kissing the lips of every bitch close enough to appreciate it. "Well, boy. Your young'un ass has just been served." I pushed the black ball into the belly of the pool table. "And that's how you do it, boy. Now pay up."

"Like I said," he said, pulling off his jacket, "we all gotta pay when we play the games, right?"

If it'd happened any faster, I'd have missed it twice over. My niggaz was sleeping and dude popped me with the burner. They hopped on him and banged it out with his other menz running for the door. Glass shattered all around, and patrons spread out on the floor and covered their heads. I just so happened to be lying on my back, spread out on my ass. The kid's aim was bad. He caught me in the shoulder. It hurt like hell, and wasn't no feeling like it.

"Come on, nigga." One of the wolves pulled me to my feet. "Can you walk?"

"I'm good." I yelped in pain.

As we ran out the door into the parking lot, cars revved up and high beams influenced the transparent falling rain, illuminating the summer teardrops. The wolves pounded out my fly-by-night shooter, dragging dude out the door into the back by his feet and leaving him for dead. Other arguments ensued, echoing off the stonewall buildings around us.

I jumped into a car one of my wolves was driving and bounced. Cars sped by us and beeped from behind as all the witnesses from the scene desperately tried to disappear before trouble appeared with the questioning and interrogation.

Nobody wanted to be anywhere around when the pigs started trying to find seven eyewitnesses to tell some news.

"You wanna go to the hospital, man?" my dude asked.

"I can't. Just get me home. Anybody know who that kid was?" I was moving back and forth in my seat in pain.

"Naw. We gonna find out though. The hospital closer than your house. You sure?"

"Yo, I said my house, nigga. Let's just work with that, a'ight."

He looked at me as if he wanted to say something but seemed to understand my position. "Yeah. A'ight, man. Home."

Chapter Forty-three

Mack

"Oh my God, Mack," Joi and Cakes exclaimed as I walked through the front door bleeding. "What happened to him?" Joi asked dude as he sat me on the couch.

"What you think happened? He got shot," he said as they all helped me pull off my jacket.

"Cakes, get a towel out the closet," Joi said. "Let me take a look at it, baby."

"Damn, baby. Take it easy," I said as Joi tugged my arm.

"I'm just trying to look at it," she said, pulling my shirt sleeve down.

"Did it go through?" I looked down at it.

"Stop moving so I can see." She backed away and began to laugh.

"What's so funny? I'm shot and you laughing?"

"You're not shot. You was grazed, man." She continued laughing.

The wolf that drove me said, "Aw, man, you a lucky dude."

"Shit hurt like hell."

"You scared us for a minute." Cakes kissed my cheek and wrapped a wet towel around my arm.

"A'ight, my man, good looks for getting me here. I want you to get in touch with Gordy and find out where he been. This here ain't gonna ride."

Cakes walked him to the door and let him out.

"Baby, you need to go upstairs and shower. I'll be up there in a sec."

"Naw, I'm good."

"You sure?"

"Yo, I said I'm good."

I was in Phenomenon's office the next night looking through the books when the door opened.

Gordy walked in with his head freshly shaven. "What's up, gangsta?"

"Look what the cat dragged in," I said standing up. "You cold fell off the radar. Where you been?"

He looked at my bandaged arm. "I been around. How you been?"

"I needed you."

"Naw, you didn't need me. You doing fine by yourself. You got your bitches on smash and respect." He chuckled.

"What's good with all the animosity?"

"Ain't nothing good with it. I'm just here to tell you I'm bouncing. I can't fuck with you no more."

"So bounce then," I said as my phone rang. "Yeah," I said, looking at Gordy.

"Mack, this is Coke."

"Yo," I calmly answered.

"How things going?"

"I'm doing good, holding it down. When you coming back?"

"Soon. I'm still taking care of some business."

"You been gone for three months. You gonna tell me what's going on?"

"Nigga, I'm out," Gordy said.

"There's a lot of shit going on you don't understand."

"Make me understand. Why you been in hiding, missing in action and what not?"

"We can't rap about that over the lines. I'll be home tomorrow, sometime after twelve A.M. I hope you had fun."

"Fun? What you talking about?"

"I'll talk to you tomorrow, pimp," he said, ending the call.

"Coke's coming home tomorrow," I said to Cakes when I got home.

I walked past her bedroom into mine.

"What?" She followed me into my room. "When you speak to him?"

"Earlier. And that bitch, Gordy, broke out. He said he ain't down no more."

"And you just let him leave?"

"Fuck 'im," I said, waving my hand.

"No, not fuck 'im. Does Coke know?"

"Fuck Coke. I'm not worried about him. I'm running this shit now. He don't got say in nothing no more."

"You serious?" she said. "You don't want to cross him, trust me."

"Bitch, I did time with the nigga. I know him a lot better than you do."

"So it's like that now? I'm a bitch?"

"Cakes, the only reason why I showed you love was on the strength of Coke. I done lost respect for the nigga. He been fucking with the cops. Like he tryin'a set me up or some shit."

"Set you up for what? What you gotta lose if you go down?"

"I worked hard to run this shit the way I have. I built shit that nigga never even thought of. I'm that young nigga he used to have inside him."

Cake looked on in astonishment, almost impressed by my defiant attitude toward the man that brought me aboard. Not too many people wanted to get into it with Coke. You know, with the crew of wolves and all, nobody really wanted that problem. But me? I had new wolves, faithful niggaz that treasured the money they was paid to protect me and the business. Our family name. The family game. So fuck Coke and all of what he did for me.

She walked closer to me. "Why are you talking like that?"

"Because I fucking mean it." I stared into her eyes. "Where's Joi?" I looked over her shoulder.

"She went out earlier last night. I ain't seen her since."

"Oh yeah? You think she out turning?"

"That ain't none of my business. But I don't see why you didn't let me do my thing. Shit, all that time Coke been gone I coulda been making it happen."

"Didn't I hold your black ass down? You never went to bed hungry and you got clothes. What else you needed? That's all a bitch need is money and clothes. You living in a house you ain't got to pay for. You drive the truck. You get the same privileges as Joi. And she my bitch. So what in the fuck could you have been lacking?"

"You really wanna know?"

"Shit. I'm asking."

"You."

"What?"

"You what I've been lacking."

I backed away as she moved closer. "I don't get what you saying."

"Do you know how long I've been wanting to fuck you?" she asked, cupping my crotch.

"You bugging." I pushed her away. "If Coke knew about this he'd kill me. He'd kill us."

"But you pimp of the year. You can do what you want. Shit. Don't think I ain't see the way you used to look at me whenever Coke turned his head. I know you like the way I used to spread that strawberry-scented lotion all over my legs before going out. Or when I wore them tight acid-wash poom-poom shorts with the holes cut out of the ass. I know you wanted to touch it. Who wouldn't? I got a sexy ass." She rubbed my hand slowly up and down it.

"This ain't right." I looked at her then out to the hallway. "I can't do that to Joi," I said, pulling my hand off her ass.

"Oh, so you gonna act like a li'l bitch because some other trick got you sprung? Because that's all it is. You in love with a stripper, a ho, a whore, all that shit."

"Get the fuck outta my house. Pack your shit, bitch."

She moved in and forced a kiss upon me that made me submit. As I backed against the wall, she pressed her face into mine. She pulled her boy shorts off, and her buttocks jiggled as they bounced out of the comfortable, cotton container for plump ass. She placed my hand back on it, sliding it up and down, and between her crack.

She sat and moved her body back and forth as our tongues continued tying knots around one another. She stepped back and pulled her shirt over her head. Her huge tits competed with one another for my affection. She pushed me to the bed, and her hardening nipples settled inside my mouth. Her three-month hiatus away from sexual activity seemed to increase her desire to be quickly and roughly penetrated.

As she positioned herself doggy-style, I quickly moved in and showed no mercy. The headboard of my bed banged against the wall like "lunch table freestyle."

She shouted and raved how bad she'd always wanted it, praising the length and width of the cable being installed inside of her.

I turned onto my back, and she mounted me, at first starting off with a slow stroll and quickly gaining momentum. She stretched, bent backwards, and rode it like she was trying to have a baby. Her excitement drenched my thighs as she bounced up and down off of them.

Just as I was about to climax, she jumped off and wrapped her mouth around it. My back arched off the bed as I growled out loudly, grabbing her head and pushing it down. She gagged and angled it more toward her right cheek, gripping the base of it and drinking my release, while jerking it up and down.

"So . . . was it good?" she asked after we rolled around on the bed for another forty-five minutes.

"You was cool," I said, getting up and pulling up my boxers.

"Cool enough to work for you?"

"Work for me? I don't know about that one, Cakes."

"Why not? You know I'd bring that paper to the table."

"I already got enough problems. You being in the mix will only make things worse."

"What you talking about? Coke?"

"Naw. Fuck him. I'm just not with that idea."

"What? You scared? I thought you was in charge. The man!"

"Oh, don't get it twisted. I am the man."

"Yeah?" she said, pulling her shirt back on. "Don't sound like it to me. Sound more like you scared what Coke will do to you when he finds out. I thought you was about paper, Mack. No, my bad. You is about paper, but only if it's just for you."

"We better get out this room before Joi come home and be thinking some shit." I walked to the door. "Fix that bed."

Chapter Forty-four

Gordy

"So why'd you want to meet with us?" Detective Jeff said to me as he and Bobby sat down to lunch inside Gino's Pizzeria in Bed-Stuy, Brooklyn.

I looked back out at my new BMW, the windows down and the music playing. I was parked right behind them in the "No Standing Anytime" zone.

"They always comes a-runnin' when the shit get thick." Bobby dumped a mound of garlic on his eggplant parmesan hero.

"I'm not running to anything."

"Then what'd you call for? You looking to make a deal before you end up in jail with the rest of your people," Jeff said.

"Naw. But I got something for you, if you can give something to me."

"Hear this guy." Jeff laughed. He almost choked on his cup of Pepsi. "What in the fuck could you possibly have for me?"

"You want Mack, right?"

Jeff looked up at me and gestured for me to carry on.

"Before you say any more, tell me what you want."

I thought about it for a sec before answering. I mean, this was it. I was fucking with the Ds, something I'd sworn to myself I'd never do. But what was I gonna do? My career was going nowhere with Mack around. And if I killed him, everybody would be looking at me. It wasn't a secret that I had no love for the nigga. Only to him.

"I want to run the ship now. My brother's too old and played-out to run shit anymore. And Mack is just taking up space. That's why he's not locked up now. Y'all ain't got nothing on him, but he keep on talking."

"How do you know we don't have anything on him?" Bobby said, wiping his mouth with a napkin.

"Because he don't do enough to attract your attention. What you really got on him? He work with my brother? So what?"

"That's all we need."

"Bullshit. I can give you some concrete shit."

"We're going to have to pass on your offer. We don't need you."

"Remember that shooting at the White Castle in Hempstead? Happened about two months ago or so."

"You know what he's talking about, Bob?"

"I remember that. They never found the shooter. What do you know about it?"

"I know who did it."

"Do you know?" Jeff rubbed his chin. "So?"

"If I give you that, what you got for me? It better be good, because I know a lot more shit than that."

"I know who killed Stan. His grandmother. You know that old bitch out in Mount Vernon. Yeah, I know all of that."

"Since you know so much and you're so anxious to make a deal with us, why not spill some shit about big brother?"

"My brother?"

Jeff said, "Yeah, your brother, you know, the big, pimp-looking muthafucka. Shit, you should want to spill something. You wouldn't have to be here bitching if there was nothing to spill. And anything you give on Mack will just lead back to your brother anyway. It's time to think about yourself now because when shit goes down everybody goes down. Unless you can give us something big. Like that shipment of your brother's coming in on Friday. Where's it going to be docking in at? What's he got on there?"

"Yeah, why not tell us that?"

"I don't know shit about no shipment."

"Come on, Gordy. You mean to tell me that baby brother to the most well-known pimp in New York City, OPT founder, don't know nothing about a shipment? Come on, whadda ya think . . . that we was born this morning, punk?"

"Yo, I swear I don't know shit about no shipment."

"It sounds convincing, Gord," Bobby said, "but my detective instincts tells me you're not being straight with us."

"They're wrong. I'm just here to see Mack go down legally. Fuck, if the pigs kill him, that'll be what's up too."

"I just don't get it." Jeff scratched his head. "Why are you here again?" he said, collecting his garbage before standing.

"Know what? Fuck it. I thought y'all liked snitches," I said out of anger. I began walking out with the two detectives behind me.

"Which way ya going?" Bobby said.

"Far the fuck away from y'all," I said, stepping into my car.

"Hey, Gord," Jeff said, "you're not too smart. You're talking all out loud about illegal activities in a public restaurant. You don't know whose ears is open. We do want to talk to you. You name the next place and time. We need solid proof of anything you give, or there is no deal. Oh yeah, if I find out you was lying about not knowing anything about that shipment tomorrow night, you won't live to regret it."

Chapter Forty-five

Cocaine

"Yeah, Mack, this Coke," I said through my cell on the way back to New York. "I'ma hit you soon as I get out the damn tunnel." I left a message on his voice mail as I entered the long tubular-shaped tunnel.

When I got outside the quick transition from darkness to light halfway blinded me. I pulled over to the side to relax my eyes for a while. I speed-dialed Mack's number again.

"Yo, what up, nigga? Where your ass been hiding?" he said.

"I ain't been hiding nowhere, but I think you need to start. The wolves will change they mind about you once I get back. You don't have a friend in the world."

"Nigga, neither do you. The word out on your ass. You had Ton kill those two cops and he's talking all about it."

"Really? From what I'm hearing, you seem to be doing a lot of talking too. So what you been saying? You don't know that those two detectives is on my payroll? Fool. You are not built for this. I'm gonna see you soon, nigga. Me and you is gonna have ourselves a nice, long chat."

"Fuck you, nigga. Don't even come back, or you might see a lot of problems."

"Boy, everybody must really got you fooled. You think you tough? You think that you could beat me? Me? After I taught you everything you know."

The call had dropped long ago. I had stopped looking down at the display while I was tearing into Mack's ass. He didn't call back, and he wasn't answering the phone either.

I'd made a couple of calls earlier and sent some niggas to his house. They was to bring him, Joi, and Cakes to my house in the Bronx, but I called the shit off and went to Phenomenon, where he was sure to be.

When I stepped into the club, everything shut down immediately. The lights came on, and the music stopped. The sound of my hard-heel Stacy Adams bounced off the walls. A lot of tight-faced looks and uncertain nods of welcome home dictated Mack was right where I thought he'd be—upstairs looking down from the window.

I went straight up the steps to the door and walked in. Mack was sitting behind my desk, his feet propped up on it, and talking on the phone. He smiled for me after I walked in and signaled for me to wait. Two other wolves was inside sitting around on the couch, comparing guns. They extended five-finger pounds, simultaneously giving off glares of mutiny in the coming.

I knocked his feet off. "Man, get your feet off my fucking desk."

The swivel chair he was sitting on turned slightly as his feet dropped to the floor. His soldiers jumped up but was quickly warned when I pulled back my jacket and revealed my .38.

"Yeah, sit on down, young boys. Gimme them shits. Put 'em on the floor and kick them over there." I pointed back at the waste basket under the window. "Now get the fuck out and tell Remy not to let nobody else up here." I closed the door behind them and locked it. With my gun still locked on Mack, I pulled down the blinds to the windows. "Call downstairs and tell 'em to put the music back on," I said, aiming at him. "You been having a real good time, haven't you?" I looked around at the four cata cornered sixteen-inch flat-screen televisions he had professionally installed. "I see you did some decorating."

"Hey, you know how I do. Like shit to look official."

"So I hear you want to take my place, that you don't even like me. When I gave you the order to kill Anton, why didn't you do it?"

"Anton was my man."

"That shit don't matter. I gave you an order and you let me down."

"I let you down." He chuckled. "You let yourself down. All your people was running they mouth way before me. You an older nigga from the streets. You can't tell the difference between friend, foe, or a snitch?" He pulled his shades halfway down under his eyes. "Yeah, nigga, you let us all down. You fucking with the pigs and shit. You treat Cakes like a dog but love her at the same time."

"What the fuck Cakes gotta do with you trying to bring me down? What the fuck it gotta do with it?" I yelled, pulling back the trigger of the pearl-handled "earth-remover." "You a li'l crab-ass nigga, I should've let the inmates have their way with you when we was locked up. Where the fuck is my brother?"

"I ain't seen him like in about two, three weeks. He quit and said he was moving on. He was cramping my style anyway." Mack blew dust out of his index fingernail. "You going to kill me?"

"Any reason why I shouldn't?"

"Two reasons."

"Oh yeah? What's that?"

"I know where Anton and Sade is holed up at. We can get them together. Ain't no more witnesses after that." He said it like he'd just solved some kind of mystery.

"There's you, and there's Joi. You might think that I won't kill you or that any nigga downstairs I snap my fingers at won't, but I'm here to let you know, Pimping. No good." I shook my head back and forth. "No good at all. Between you and Anton, y'all both got them pigs up my ass. Where's Cakes?"

"At the house with Joi."

"It's about time for that bitch to come on home. What you think?"

"I think you think how you think. Get her nigga. Do you."

"You lucky I got love for you, Mack, but I'm really disappointed in you."

"I got us a building full of bitches. I did that on my own. I can run this shit."

"No, you can't. I got here by climbing ladders. You here on my back about to slip off and slide down the chute." I put my shit back into its holster. "Get up, nigga. Let's go. Cocaine is back in town, and shit is gonna be different from now on."

We both slowly walked down the steps as if nothing happened. Both sides of new and old wolves watched us as we walked out to the parking lot.

"Everything good, y'all?" Remy said. He was our young, six-feet six, 320-pound bouncer.

"It's all good, son," Mack said. "Hold it down for a while. I'll be back in about an hour or two."

"Goddamn, Coke. This you?" Mack said when we got to the parking lot. He ran his hand across the hood of my silver Jaguar. "When you get this?"

"Just get in your car so we can leave," I said, making a call as I sat behind the steering wheel of my car.

Mack's truck roared to life as he backed out on the edge of the exit. "I'm following you, or you following me?" He smiled out his window.

"Follow me."

We get to Mack's house, and Cakes is on the porch with Joi holding shopping bags. She dropped them the second she saw my face through the passenger window.

"Get over here," I told her.

She slowly approached with a withering smile. "Hi, daddy," she said, kissing my lips through the window.

"What's with all the bags? Are those yours?" I nodded toward the porch.

"I needed something to wear. I can't just go around wearing the same ol' shit every day."

Right away I knew Mack had gotten into her head. She never spoke to me like that in a very long time because she knew I'd give her a smack. Which is exactly what happened the instant she let the last word escape her mouth.

Mack parked behind me and hopped down out of his truck.

"Get in the car, Cakes. We're going home."

She held on to the side of her face and looked back to Mack.

Joi said from the porch, "You all right, Cakes?"

"Cakes, get your ass in this car before I really have to embarrass your ass."

"You don't gotta go nowhere, Cakes." Mack grabbed her arm. "Why don't you chill out, Coke? You don't got to be putting your hands on her."

I stepped out my Jag. "What?"

"I said you don't got to be putting your hands on her."

Cakes stepped behind him as if he was some sort of protection.

"Just take it easy," he said, his hand on my chest.

"Oh, take it easy? Cakes, if you know what's good for you, your ass better come on so we can go. One, two—"

Before I could get to three, she slowly stepped from behind Mack and walked toward the passenger door.

"That's what it is now, boy? You trying to control my bitch too? My property? I said to get your black ass in the car." I banged on the hood.

"Hold up, Cakes. You don't got to do anything you don't want to do. Go on back in the house with Joi."

She hesitated, looking back and forth between us both. Lights in the windows of darkened houses began flicking on from all the commotion we were stirring up.

"You take a step toward that porch and it'll be the last thing you ever do." I looked at her over the roof of the car. "Go ahead. I dare ya."

"Go on, Cakes. You ain't got shit to worry about."

She turned her head on me and proceeded walking away from me and toward Mack.

"See, bruth, I told you. Your time is over." Mack wrapped his arm around Cakes. "Cakes is about making her paper. You keep taking her shit. That ain't good business."

"What in the hell you know about good business, huh?" I got up in his face. "Just what do you know? Nothing you is doing was done on your own. This is my shit! I'm not letting you fuck it up."

"Naw, this my shit, and that's what it is."

"You don't know what you getting yourself into, boy. You think that my people really got love for you? Yeah, you made some new friends and money while I was away, but it don't mean shit. You know how long I been doing this for? These streets will eat your frail ass alive. You ain't been through nothing. What the fuck you been through? Cakes, I'm not gonna try and stop you. You go ahead and leave with this nigga if you want to. Just tell me one thing—Is he gonna take care of you the way I have? Is he ever gonna love you officially the way I have?" I asked passionately as I walked toward her.

"Go 'head on in the house," Mack said to her. "And is he gonna care about you like a father?"

She stood still looking back and forth at us. Trapped in a dilemma, tears began forming at the bottom of her lids. They sparkled under the bright street lights, hit the ground, then splashed.

I held out my hand. "Cakes, come on back home. It's not a request. You know who loves you. Look at that nigga. Do it look like he can protect anything?"

Mack walked toward me. "You're not going to keep disrespecting me, my man."

"And what the fuck you gonna do, huh? You don't wanna fuck with me. But I dare ya," I said, four feet of animus space between us two.

Two seconds later we became one, dancing like wolves in a concrete forest of street lamps, expensive parked cars, and recyclable garbage cans.

"Stop it, y'all," Joi yelled from the porch. "Y'all gonna have the police out here."

"You li'l shit," I said, my arm locked around his neck, "you're a fucking zero. Bitch! Your whole life is about to change."

He scooped me off my feet and stumbled backwards. We hit the ground hard and heavy. Fists swung in fury, nothing shielding our faces from the sharp blows we exchanged.

"Stop it," Cakes yelled out, standing over us. "Just stop it! Coke, I'll come home with you. I'll come home."

Joi walked to the middle of the street and gave Cakes a hug as Mack and I stood facing one another eye to eye.

"Let's go inside, Mack." Joi wiped the tears from Cakes' face. "You gonna be all right, girl. We had fun together," she said, hugging her.

"Remember, nigga," I said, pointing to Mack, "you started this." I sat in the car and waited for Cakes to get in and screeched off down the road before she could strap her seat belt on.

Chapter Forty-six

Mack

Before Cakes could strap herself into her seatbelt Coke had already slapped her in the face five times before screeching off down the road.

"What was you thinking?" Joi said as we walked into the house. "You fighting for Cakes? His woman?"

"She's not his woman, she's his personal punching bag."

"And what part of the game is it when you make that your business? What Cake getting her ass beat by her pimp got to do with you?"

"I saved your ass from a life of 'beats and production,' didn't I?"

"What the fuck that gotta do with you out in the street fighting for another woman? Do you know how fucked up that looks?"

"I wasn't fighting for her. I was fighting for us. You and me. Cakes wanted to roll with me. My new team. I told her I'd put her on."

"Right under Cocaine's nose, right? Don't we got enough problems with him as it is? Then you wanna tell his woman to stay . . . with me standing right there. Why you trying to be something you not? You need to stop before this goes any further. The ride was fun. We got paid. We got the money from the house in Mount Vernon. Stan is dead. You been making all of Coke's money while he been away. You proved yourself. All right, already. This pimping ain't for you, Mack, trust me. I've seen a lot and done a lot with you and for you. It's not in your blood. Let's just take what we got and bounce, babe."

"I don't even know why I cleaned your silly ass up. You not standing by my side."

"You damn right. Not when the dumb shit you doing can get me killed. Or a lifetime sentence in prison. You must think those Ds forgot all about us. Your li'l girlfriend Sade and homeboy Anton is fien'in' to be some free birds once they can prove something concrete. Why sit around waiting on chance? Let's just leave."

"Know what"—I grabbed her by the arm—"Why don't *you* just leave." I shoved her out the door.

"Oh, that's fucked up." She began crying. "You ain't never threw Sade out."

"Sade was a real woman. You ain't nothing but a money-hungry ho. The fuck outta here, trick," I said, slamming the door shut in her face.

She pounded on the door and yelled, "I want my money and clothes, Mack."

I jerked it open, pulled her in, and flung her to the floor. She rolled over into the coffee table and hit her head on the wooden leg.

Joi was the only one left I thought I could trust. But she was just like the rest of them. Nobody wanted to see a nigga shine and be successful and shit.

She looked up, holding the side of her head. "What you doing?"

"I'm not a real pimp? I'm not a real pimp?" I smacked her repeatedly on the top of her head. "Who the hell takes care of you?" I ran over to the blinds and closed them as she tried crawling toward the staircase. I grabbed her by the leg and dragged her across the living room floor and into the kitchen.

"Mack, stop."

"Mack, stop what," I said, slapping her face. "Mack stop what." I tapped her in the forehead with my ring finger. "You're my bitch, and you're not going to disrespect me, you understand?" I kicked her in the stomach. "You don't question anything I ever do, or the next time you can just hop off that porch and run for your life because I ain't playing games no more."

Joi lay on the floor covered up to protect herself from my assault.

I mean, these bitches had to learn that when a pimp is talking, you're not supposed to be. Play your position is what I'm saying. I left her right there on the kitchen floor, washed my ass, then went to bed.

Chapter Forty-seven

Mack

"Wake up, nigga!" a ski-masked dude yelled. He had four others next to him as I lay comfortably in bed. My eyes slowly opened to a gun pointed at my head.

"Yeah, wake your fake ass up, stupid."

I raised my hands in the air and looked at the other masked men. They had Joi bound with duct tape around her mouth and wrists. Her left eye was blackened, and she had bloodstains on her white bra and panty set. She tried resisting one of them, only to be shaken and slammed into the wall where she dropped.

"You see that shit, Pimping," the masked dude holding the gun on me said. "That's what happens to snitches. You should've left when you had the chance, acting like you running something. You's about to be one dead pimp. Get this nigga up out the bed," he said to his menz.

Before jerking me off the bed, they put a pounding on me then took turns raping Joi into unconsciousness. They dragged her out the house while I was held at bay with the gun.

"Cocaine said to come see him or this bitch is dead as you are." He banged me in the head with the butt of his gun.

Everything began to spin around, and I lost vision.

When I awoke, my room was in shambles, Joi was gone, and police sirens flashed down below outside of my window. Red spinning lights flickered against the wall in my darkened bedroom. I used its guiding light to lead me down what felt like a story of steps. I fell against the front door before opening it. I turned the knob, opened it, and stumbled out down the four sets of stairs before me.

An officer yelled from behind his squad car, "Stop where you are."

Three police vehicles was parked in the middle of the street, while two sat up on the curb of the sidewalk. Distorted signals of distress calls cried out through the squad car windows and squealed out from the pigs with radios attached to their belt clips, radios used more times than many to subdue a resisting victim with way too much melanin in his skin. I was fortunate enough to escape the frequencies of a transmitted ass-whupping and was just simply tased with the same amount of watts that shocked the shit out of Rodney King while the LAPD beat the West Coast out of his can't-we-all-just-get-along ass.

"I'm the victim, man," I said, shaken.

The burning tires of a dark blue Intrepid screeched up on to the curb. An early morning crowd of witnesses began gathering all along the street, sidewalk, and bay windows of startled residents who hadn't seen this much action since O.J.'s high-profile, slow-speed police chase.

The cocky officer aimed the taser at me. "Stop moving around before I zap you again."

"I didn't do anything," I said, struggling with the blood flow-blocking handcuffs tightly locked around my wrists.

As I quietly lay on my stomach on the sidewalk in front of my house, two sets of feet walked up and stopped. Jeff kneeled down beside me. "My main man Mack, looks like your ass been tased, homeboy."

"What's going on? I ain't do nothing. I was assaulted in my own house and they took my girl," I said, talking to him with the side of my face down on the ground.

"Oh yeah? Well, we got an anonymous tip that you set it all up because your bitch was cheating on you."

"That's bullshit and you know it."

"Hey, I don't know shit, just like you don't know shit. I told you you'd need me one day. You really should've talked when you had the chance. Now look at you. Say, officer," he said to the rookie, "what's the charge?"

"Break-in and entry."

"Break-in and entry? That's my fucking house. You can ask anyone standing out here. I live here. Tell 'em, detective," I said to Jeff.

"Tell 'em what?"

"That this is my house. How the fuck am I going to break in my own house? What I'm going to do, rob myself?"

Another officer pulled me up by the arm. "Stand up."

"Y'all been to my house before. You sat on my couch, both of you. Why y'all fronting?" I looked at Bobby and Jeff.

"Fronting? Mack, what the fuck kinda language is you talking?" Jeff said. "Bobby, you know what he's talking about?"

"Nope. Can't say I do. Thing I'm confused about is, why in the hell would you rob a house then strip down to your underwear?"

"Because I live here," I yelled.

As the other officers argued with the nosy residents, one officer said, "All right. Is that all, detectives? We're going to take him on in."

"No, that's not all. We need to talk to this guy real fast. We're going to take him over to our car. He'll be right back. Come on, you." Jeff walked me to his car. "So you still feeling like a pimp?"

"I'm feeling like this is all one big set-up."

"Know what, asshole," Jeff said, "you're right. It is one big set-up. You set yourself up when you decided you wanted to be the man. Who did this to you?" He grabbed my chin and turned my head side to side as he examined my bruise.

Bobby said, "Looks like somebody worked you over pretty good."

I turned my head. "Fuck you."

"Hey, look you. Jeff is the nice guy. You don't want to be getting tough with me. Now we know who did this and we know you know who did this. Just give the name and we'll go pick 'em up."

"Naw." I shook my head back and forth. "I don't know who did this."

"You wanna play stupid with us, Mack, that's fine. Your time is almost up. We're right on your ass. Fuck up once more and that's it. I think you oughta take a ride with us," Jeff said. "Officer, we're going to take this dick in. Have your sergeant call me. Get in the car," Jeff said, shoving me into the back seat before sitting beside me. "Hey, Mack, you know that guy waving at you across the street?"

I saw some dude waving, but he was standing in the shadows of the long, hanging branches. He stepped into the light, waving with such a look of hate on his face.

"Hey, Mack, ain't that your main man Cocaine?" Bobby said, sniffing and rubbing his nose as he said it.

Jeff laughed. "Well, I'll be a son-of-a-bitch. It is. Uh-oh, Mack. Oh, boy, does he look mad. Goddamn, boy, I thinks you is in some deep shit. Roll down that window, Bob. Hey, Cocaine, we're coming for you next," he said with his hand on my shoulder.

Cocaine smiled and continued waving, and some of his wolves began to gather into a pack. They was ready to wild out and attack at his command, while the late-night moon still was full.

"Go 'head on and drive off," I said, keeping an eye on them all.

"Why? You scared? Those your peoples, ain't they?" Jeff said.

"Drive, Bob. You know where to go."

I turned back after we drove off. Cocaine was still looking at me until we both lost sight of each other's expression of MDK. There was about to be a demolition, man. And I wasn't going to be the one at the bottom of it.

I looked around nervously as we crossed over the GWB. "Where y'all taking me?"

"We just saved your life. So, the way I see it, you owe us a favor." Bobby looked back over his shoulder

"Let me outta here. Y'all can't do this."

"Shut up. You're in some real shit. I'm going to let you know something right now—Your boy set you up. He called the police on you."

"What? He sent those dudes up in my house after me?"

"Yeah." He smiled. "Why'd he send them after you?"

"He's mad. A hater and shit."

"Oh, come on, there's gotta be a much more legit reason than that. You been stealing on his business is what I think. And when you steal on his business"—Jeff moved close to my ear—"you steal from our business." He pointed to himself and Bobby.

"How I'm stealing from you?"

Jeff said, "Look at you . . . you still don't know shit after all this time."

"What the hell are you talking about?"

"Think back to the first day you came into our office. We played you for a sucker, acting as if we didn't know what you was into. We've been watching you ever since you met up with Cocaine in prison. He works for us. Why do you think he gets away with as much as he has? We make his problems disappear for twenty percent of everything he's involved in. You're probably making less, when it's just you and him, so I can see why you'd want to venture off on your own. But you ventured a little too far off track. Enough for Internal Affairs to be watching us."

"And just enough to make Cocaine stop paying us and telling us about a bust here or there a couple of times out the month. So don't think you're the only one telling shit to save your own ass," Bobby said.

"Now how do you feel?" Jeff said.

Chapter Forty-eight

Mack

Hours later we arrived in Albany, New York at the Motel 6, a run-down piece of shit in the middle of nowhere. The sun was just coming up. We pulled into the parking lot, where another D.T. car was parked. Bobby honked the horn, and one D.T. walked out of one room and another one from the room next to it.

"What's this?" I said, staring at them as they yawned and stretched their aching backs in the doorways. "It's your sanctuary," Jeff said awakening. He had nodded off during the five-hour ride. "And your reunion."

"Reunion? What you talking about now?"

"You'll see." Bobby stepped out the car and met with his comrades halfway. "How's it going, fellas?" he said, shaking their hands. "You guys look like shit. Go get some coffee. We'll take over from here. See ya next shift."

The fatigued men slowly walked to their car and honked as they drove off. "I'm going to take those cuffs off you," Jeff said. "Try any funny business, and I won't hesitate to shoot you in the head."

After taking the cuffs off, they both walked on opposite sides of me to room twelve on the second floor.

As we entered, I fell face first onto the stiff mattress of the cheap bed. I turned over on my back and observed the rings around my wrists from the tight cuffs. "Y'all don't think those cuffs was on too tight?"

"Be happy I took them off," Jeff said. "You hungry?"

Bobby ran down to the local store and returned with coffee and a warm buttered roll. "You better eat while you can," he said. "You might not get another chance at it."

I stared down at the greasy wax paper holding the buttered roll.

Bobby said, "Now I know you've got to be wondering why we brought you here."

"Uh, yeah. The thought did cross my mind once or twice."

Jeff cuffed me to the desk and placed my coffee next to my free hand.

"What's up, man? I thought we was done with the enslavement." I tugged at the chain between the silver bracelets.

"We'll be back in a second. It's just that we can't risk you running off into the sunset before we get what we want out of you. I think you'll be more willing to talk when we get back. Come on, Bob, let's leave this guy to his bread and coffee." Jeff laughed.

The door closed behind them, and I immediately began pulling at the desk. I tugged, pulled, and jerked, but it was all in vain. The desk was bolted down onto the floor and would not give. I kept trying anyway until I was breathless and exhausted. I lay out across the floor with my arm up in the air.

Half an hour later, I was alerted by a turn of the doorknob.

"Good thing we cuffed you. Looks like you was trying to escape," Jeff said. "Look who joined the party."

Bobby walked in with Sade and Anton cuffed together behind him.

"What you gotta say now, Eric?" Jeff said with a smile.

Sade and Ton both looked at one another in total shock as I lay on the floor cuffed to the desk.

"I can tell by your reaction, kids, that you have a lot to catch up on, so me and my partner here are going to let you three discuss it. We'll be right outside the door, if you need us," Jeff said.

"Aren't you going to take these things back off?" I asked.

"No. We wouldn't want you all trying to kill each other before we have anything. You just stay right there on the floor." Bobby released Ton and Sade from their bracelets of captivity.

"What about them? Why you letting them out they cuffs?"

"Why, Mack? You scared something might happen to you? You deserve it. But we're right outside the door. Everything will be fine. Maybe they can talk some sense into your ass."

After they walked out and closed the door, Ton and Sade continued to just stare at me as I struggled for a comfortable position.

Silence consumed the room for the first ten minutes, until Jeff stuck his head through the door. "I don't hear you guys celebrating. Cheer up, Mack. It's a party." He closed the door again.

"You's a foul dude, man," Ton said, breaking the uncomfortable silence. "You done did a lot of people dirty."

"You don't know what you're talking about. I ain't never done nobody dirty that didn't deserve it."

"Oh, so I deserved it?" Sade said.

"You fucked yourself, Sade. You know if you would've told me what was going on, I would've came and got you."

"You left me to rot in prison and moved another bitch right on in when you was sure I wasn't getting out."

"You hear a lot of shit when you get locked up, Mack," Ton said. "You hear a lot of shit."

"So what you getting at?"

"Why you never warned me that Coke wanted me dead? Then, to top it all off, you was given the order to take me out. What you got to say on that?"

"Nigga, I say you're still here. I had plenty of opportunities to take you out, and I never did. I jeopardized my own life, looking out for yours."

"Did you jeopardize your life looking out for me? Where's my money?" Sade said.

"That money is spent. Had investments to make."

"Investments? With my money?"

"Our money. You was living in my house. It's our money."

"Your house?" she said. "You don't own shit, but the fear in your heart. Everything you are and have is because of Cocaine. That's his house, his money. You still riding around in his truck, acting like you put some money into that? You are a fraud."

"That sounds real funny coming from somebody who traveled all the way out of state just to kill they mother just because you can't get over a fucked-up childhood. I told you before to just let it go. And you, Ton, you acting all high and mighty. Niggas done told me how you was badmouthing me and just waiting to take my spot, you and that faggot-ass Gordy."

They took turns shooting accusations and threats at me.

"I hope it all was worth it, Mack, I really do," Sade said. "You didn't even at least try to write me. Didn't ask no one how I was. Nothing. You never loved me."

"If you ever loved me none of this would be going down now. Y'all both got my name in your mouth based on some shit y'all got caught for. I ain't had shit to do with y'all mistakes."

"That's how you gonna look at it, man," Ton said. "After all we did together? As many times as I had your back in the most fucked-up situations?"

"Did I tell you to smoke those cops? Sade, did I tell you to kill your moms?"

"Did we tell you to start snitching?" Anton said. "The word is already out. How you think

Coke got them niggas to run up in your spot? He gave that order. And know what else? Those two dicks outside, they know it. They been playing you for a fucking ass. They're gonna make you take the fall for Cocaine."

"How they gonna do that, when everything points to him?"

"Not everything. Not Stan. Not his grandmother. Not the robberies. Not the White Castle video tape you and Gordy is on."

"Payback is a bitch, Mack. I told them everything I know about you."

"If they know so much, then why I ain't in court somewhere being convicted?"

"Because they want you to work for them or take the fall. They'll make it look as if you're the mastermind behind the whole operation. That means you'll be charged with conspiracy and double homicide for putting the hit out on those pigs."

"But you did it."

"Doesn't matter. Wouldn't have happened if the order wasn't given."

"Naw, naw. Fuck that. I ain't doing nobody's time but my own. I ain't kill Stan. Joi did the shit. I ain't never kill nobody."

"What you mean, you ain't kill Stan?"

"I lied. Joi let that nigga have the lead. She hated him, wanted him gone, so she shot him."

"So you been misleading muthafuckas all this time? You hear this nigga, Sade? So Gordy wasn't being paranoid when he was trying to always pull your card?"

"Gordy's a hater. Even if I did do the shit myself he'd still find a reason not to like me. That's just how some niggas is."

"When this is all over with," Ton said, "we can't never be cool again."

"That already was the first thing on my to-do list when you got bagged."

"I can't believe I wasted a portion of my life fucking with you," Sade said.

Jeff stuck his head back in the door. "You guys all getting along?" He sipped from a Styrofoam cup full of steaming coffee. "I know how rowdy things can get when the brothers hear there's a party." He looked down at me. "Anybody get through to this knucklehead yet?"

Chapter Forty-nine

Cocaine

I figured siccing Jeff and Bobby on Mack would make them take their eyes off of my ass for a while. It was just the time I needed to go to the Hamptons and pick up my shipment.

I rented two vans that night, before me and my men left, but I wasn't going anywhere until I handled some shit with them. I stepped up on the stage inside Phenomenon and turned on the microphone, so nobody could say they missed something. "Gentlemen, what's happening?"

They all gave nods and chanted, "Chilling."

"I'll get right to what I gots to say. Anybody feeling a way about that bitch-ass Mack getting what he deserved . . . because I know a number of y'all got real close with him in my absence? Heard he was doing all types of crazy shit, and y'all was backing him. Even managed to get your pockets a little fatter. I'm not gonna go through a whole lot of changes trying to find out who got what. All I need to know is if any nigga in here still wanna roll with Mack, raise your hands." I said to one of the wolves, "What about you? You in or you out?"

"I'm good where I'm at," he said.

"That's good. Is everybody else good?"

"Naw, duke," another wolf said, "I ain't good. Mack's my dude. I thought y'all was tight like fam."

A couple more bitches participated in the treason and walked out the door. What was left was all I needed to get my business done tonight.

It was about 1:00 A.M. when we pulled up into the long driveway of the country club in both vans. The others drove their cars. There was a big billboard sign in the spacious front yard. I read the sign, "Charlie's Krackers—This is the place."

Three of my men came with me to the side door entrance. A small metal plate slid across and opened from the middle of the door.

"Password," a voice said through the opening.

"Bohemian."

The door went through several phases of mechanisms unlocking and finally opened.

The fat honky said, staring at me and my men up and down, "What is your business here?"

"I'm a friend of Craig Dudley . . . from D.C. I'm looking for Dan."

He stared for a moment longer before stepping back so we all could enter. Inside on the walls was framed pictures of championship golfers. Three old-style ceiling fans silently spun, circulating the cigar-smoke-filled room.

A white man in a white suit walked out from a back room. He was eating a piece of chicken. "Solomon," he said, extending his free hand.

I applied a firm grip. "Call me Cocaine."

His people stared at my people, and they returned duplicate looks of dislike and trust.

"So how long you've known Craig?"

"Doesn't matter. You've been paid, right?"

"Yep. All you have to do is pull them vans around back, then off you go."

"All right. Let me see what I'm working with, before I just throw some shit up in my vans."

"No problem." Then he said to the bartender, "James, get these gentlemen anything they want."

We walked out through the back door of the country club and went out around back.

Dan pulled out a key and slipped it into the groove of the door's lock. "You're going to make back triple what you paid me to make this happen."

"Oh, I already know that. Especially since I've gotten rid of my deadweight."

He slowly pushed open the door to the dark room. Shuffling feet inside put me on alert, and I reached for my gun.

"Whoa," he said, pushing my hand down. "We just scared them. Relax."

I placed my gun back behind my waist and waited for him to find the light switch. I smiled when the lights came on. Huddled up together naked against the wall was twelve illegal immigrant South African girls ranging in ages twelve to fourteen. Dollar signs lit up in my eyes when it registered in their heads that I was about to become their new master.

A couple of years back I'd heard through the grapevine that there was a ship that came into New Jersey carrying South African minors sold into slavery by their parents to make ends meet. They'd been in his barn for about three weeks. My white clients would pay top dollar to fuck just one of those young and tender beauties from the Motherland. I'd clean them up just like I'd done the rest of the hoes and put them straight to work. Best thing of all is, I wouldn't have to do anything but feed and clothe them. I was gonna change the game.

I walked over to one of them that was holding on tightly to the arm of what appeared to be her sister. I felt on her blossoming chest then smoothed my hand down her overdeveloped ass.

She said something in her native language. I was guessing that it meant no.

"She's a feisty one," Dan said, "but her apple is sweet as pie." He stuck his finger up in her then licked it. "Mmm . . . so sweet. She's an investment to look forward to. All of them are."

I watched him as he took pride in admitting his pedophile ways. Salivating from the corners of his mouth, he stared wide-eyed at each and every last one of them .

"So how do I know these girls clean, man?" I asked.

"Got all their medical records inside. They're all clean."

"All right. Let's get that going then so I can get these bitches out of here. They need showers and a meal. They looking a little malnourished."

"They're all yours. Do what you want with them. Just get them niggers the hell out of here. Let me bring that paperwork out for you."

We put six girls in each van and wrapped their naked bodies with blankets. The tinted windows on the van prevented the wandering eyes of distracted, parkway drivers from looking in on our operation.

Chapter Fifty

Mack

It had been a week since I was kidnapped by these clowns. At the end of the day all they wanted me to do was testify and it'd be all over. We'd all go free, long as we did exactly what they said. They really was on some shady shit because they had picked me up for Cocaine, telling him that if he got the money thing right with them again, then everything that was pending on us both would all fall on me.

Jeff and me went down to the first floor, where there was a door already open to the motel. Jeff pulled up a chair and had me sit at the foot of the bed. "Eric, you don't mind if I use the name your mother gave you at birth, do you?"

I shrugged my shoulders. "Whatever, man."

"Don't you want to go home and take a long, hot shower? You've got to be tired of seeing our faces. Especially Anton's and Sade's. You know they hate you, right? Tell ya what, I wouldn't want to be sitting in a room full of hate."

"Why you always start off with this mind-fucking shit, man? Just get to the fucking point."

"All right. Before I do, I'm going to do you a favor."

"Yeah? Like what?"

"I'm going to remove those cuffs so we can talk like men. Try any funny shit and I'll shoot you right in the head." He stuck the key down into the cuffs lock. "Now I want you to talk to me about everything. We've been through this before. Let me help you help yourself."

"Talk," I said, rubbing my wrists.

"Cocaine is going down. Matter of fact, we don't give a shit about you. But we don't have enough solid proof to get something on him without witnesses. Once we have a conviction, you can take over where he left off. Long as you pay on time, we won't bother you. You can pimp all the hoes you want to, but you gotta give me something on that fuckhead. I know you like that idea. No more looking over your shoulder."

"If I do this, and I'm not saying I am, will you really be able to get Sade and Anton off completely? I mean totally?

"Eric, my man, scout's honor." He stuck up his two fingers.

"Naw, not good enough. I wanna see the shit on paper and signed by the D.A."

"There's one more thing."

"What's that?"

"Joi. We know she killed Stan, but who killed his grandmother? Somebody has to take the fall for that. Now if you can give us something else to overshadow that, then she can get off too."

"Yeah. Only thing is, Coke had her kidnapped. For all we know, she could be dead now."

"She's not."

"How you know?"

"We needed to question her again, so we set up the kidnapping."

"Go on." I rubbed my chin in mad suspicion.

"Coke's men don't really trust him anymore. They feel he's getting too old for this. He wanted to know what she knows and paid us to send people up in there. He's under the impression he still has us in his pocket."

"So those wasn't his men?"

"They were, but only in his mind. Everybody's looking for a deal to save their own ass. They'll testify in court that he had her kidnapped."

"So where's she at now?"

"She's safe."

"How I know you not setting me up? Like, we all give you everything you need then flip the script on us?"

"I like making money just like you. If you can keep up the good work you did in his absence, then there's no reason why you'll have to worry about that."

"Like I said, I want it in writing. For all of us."

"Not a problem. You just write down on this pad," he said passing me the yellow lined paper. "Write everything. Between you and Anton and Sade, it should be enough to get a conviction."

"And I can go back to being the man?"

"You can go back to being that nigger."

"I think I like the sound of that." I smiled.

"So do we have a deal, Eric?"

"Yeah. Just one more thing though," I said.

"Anything for my nigger."

"Call me Mack."

"Deal. Shake on it?" He held out his hand.

I momentarily contemplated my options once over then gave in. "Deal," I said, shaking his hand.

"My nigger." He smiled.

Chapter Fifty-one

Cocaine

With Mack gone, everything was just about back to normal again. The building he went and bought behind my back was still running. Friday nights was still a big moneymaker at Phenomenon. I was home and back in the driver's seat. I even started letting Cakes go out on the weekends to shop for new clothes with the other girls. The girls from South Africa wasn't allowed to leave the house under any circumstances. Only my high-paying professional clients could touch them. None of them spoke a word of English, so it was easy to control them. And when they didn't listen or a client complained about unsatisfactory services they'd be penalized with a severe ass-whupping. If one of them fucked up, then they all got beat. I used them to keep the house clean. Cook the meals for clients before they came. Yeah, that was my idea. Why not have some fried chicken and sweetbread out? Hoes and clients had to be hungry after all that fantasizing and fucking.

"I don't feel good," Cakes said, dragging her feet across the living room.

I was looking out the Venetian blinds. "You don't look good either."

"I'm serious. Something's wrong."

"Like what, Cakes? I don't have time for this. It's going to be a busy night."

"I need to go to the emergency room. I feel sick."

"Look, I put you back to work, so don't start up with no bullshit. You working tonight from eight 'til two. This is what you wanted."

"I understand all that, but if I'm sick, I'm sick," she said, rolling her eyes.

"I really don't give a shit how sick you is, woman. You my moneymaker. Make that shit happen. If you still sick tomorrow, I'll take you to the doctor myself."

"Whatever, Coke. I'm going to lie down before I get dressed. Don't say shit when one of the clients say I threw up on their dick."

"That's the spirit. Do that freaky shit. That'll keep 'em coming back."

I was already near the house phone, when I picked it up on the first ring. "Hello?"

"Hello. This is the operator. You have a collect call from Glen, will you accept the charges?"

What the fuck does he want now? I paid his child-support issue, put money in his commissary. See, that just goes to show that you can't do shit for a nigga without him holding out his hand for more. But I wanted to be amused, so I took the call.

"Solomon, hey, man, I really appreciate what you did for me."

"It's nothing, but look here, me and you is done. I got too much going on for a nigga from prison to be calling my house. So who was the bitches that filed the cases against you?"

"They didn't do it. Welfare did it. I got two grown-ass kids running around out there and don't know who they is."

"That's real crazy."

"Yeah. Well, what the fuck you gonna do, man?"

"I don't know what you're gonna do, but I myself have a lot of business to take care of, so you take care of yourself, cuz. Sorry it got to be this way, but I told you a long time ago about dealing with all them bitches. Now look where it done landed you at."

"This is all that damn Sade's fault. You ain't heard where they hiding that bitch out at yet, man?"

"Look, don't be talking crazy over the lines. And, naw, I ain't heard shit. Take your medicine like a man, Glen. You fucked up. The bitch beat you to the punch."

"This not even fair. I can't do no twenty-five years."

"Then maybe you should've thought about that before you let some bitch put you in the mix."

"I'm not doing this time by myself. She gonna pay."

"All right, I'm about to go. Stop calling here collect. Matter of fact, stop calling here altogether. You're gonna make my shit hot. I did all I can do for you."

"Not all. You know what I really need for you to do."

I disconnected the call before he started talking that "offing Sade" shit again. I had enough problems with them other muthafuckas trying to get me knocked. But as long as I could keep paying those two pigs their money, they'd hold on to all three of them. Boy, did they ever have Mack fooled, having him believe if he told on me they'd put him on top. He had no idea they was calling me every day, telling me every bit of information he said. The only reason why he wasn't dead yet was because I didn't need him dead yet. I needed him to take the fall when shit really did go down. If he really wanted to run this, he was going to suffer the consequences that came along with it. More important than that, I needed to find out where in the hell my brother disappeared to. He had some shit that could fuck up everybody, no matter how much of an ass he made Mack look like in the end.

Tonight was turning out to be one of the best nights making money I'd had in years. These little bitches had to be the best idea I ever thought of. They became such a hot commodity, because their bodies had not yet experienced the wear and tear of aging, the older bitches started becoming jealous. The men loved them and the fact that their young tunnels of submissiveness provided a tight squeeze, as opposed to the older women, who at times were loose, sloppy, and stank. I had to let a couple of them go. I put Cakes in charge of keeping the young girls presentable. She became sort of like their house mother, keeping them nourished, clothed, and clean.

"I don't know if I like the idea of pimping these babies, daddy," Cakes said.

"It's not your job to not like what I tell you to do. You just do the shit. I don't pay you to think. If I did, we'd all be out on the street."

"One of the girl's is looking sickly. She needs to go to the hospital."

"Just like you needed to go the other night, right? I don't understand this. Y'all is off the street. A place to live, no problems in the street with nobody. What else y'all want from me? Why everybody trying to find a reason to desert me? All I've done is give, give, and give."

"If you talking about me so, what you give, give, give? You think this is something I wanna be doing for the rest of my life? You really think I wanna look back at my life and tell my kids the only thing that mommy was ever good at was keeping her legs cocked open?"

"I tell you what, Cakes, we all gotta be good at something. You're good at what you do, just like I'm good at what I do. You're the company, and I'm the management. We not gonna be doing this here forever. But I need you to do what you do best, so we can keep getting that money. Then one day me and you can live in the lap of luxury. I'd never ask you to turn another trick again. You know you my number one superstar. I may not always act like it, but I'm under so much stress. I only yell at you because we in a business where there ain't room for mistakes. You can understand that, right?"

"I do understand that. I just wish you'd let me give my two cents every once in a while. You make me feel like I'm not shit sometimes," she said, looking toward the floor.

"Hey, you making me feel like I'm not shit right now." I lifted her chin. "Out of every last one of these bitches that work for me, who I show the most love and respect to, huh?"

"Me."

"And who I trust with the books?"

"Me."

"Uh-huh. Who I let sit up in here and didn't have to fuck not one nigga for months?"

"Me." She shyly looked on before letting her head drop back down.

"So don't you think you being just a bit unfair to me by saying I don't listen to you? Just look around you, Cakes. You got it real good. Not every pimp can provide you with a home like this. I've been like your father, your lover, your best friend, the only person in the world looking out for your best interest. And don't forget who paid for your mother to get into that drug rehab program."

"You right. You've done mad shit for me. I just want a little something that I can get on my own. I wanna feel adequate."

"You *are* adequate. When all this is over, we're gonna get married in the Bahamas. Now I know I been promising you that forever, but this time I'm serious. Things is different now. You won't have to do this for much longer. You trust me, right?"

"Yeah. Who else do I have? What else do I have? Where else do I have to go?"

"You don't have to go nowhere. You're already where you belong."

She threw her arms around my neck and clung on tight. She looked up at me and kissed my cheek then dropped to the floor.

"Cakes," I exclaimed, immediately falling by her side, "Cakes, quit playing." I shook her shoulder as she moaned.

"I don't feel so good."

I ran back over to the phone and dialed nine-one-one.

Chapter Fifty-two

Cocaine

I followed behind the speeding ambulance, dipping in and out of traffic. I parked in the handicapped zone and ran in the double sliding doors of the emergency room. I was directed into the rear of the hospital and told to wait. An hour later, I was called into an office by a doctor. "So what's the matter with her, doc?" I said to him as we stood outside the room Cakes was resting in. "Well, I'm sorry to have to be the one to tell you this." He looked down at his medical chart.

"Don't be sorry and don't bullshit me. What's the problem?" I snatched the chart from him. "What this all here mean?"

"Do you want to talk inside?" he said, opening the door. "Let's go. Cakes, how you doing?" I said, holding her hand. She had her back turned to us both. "Ms. Donavon," he called to her, "are you all right?" She slowly turned over to face us both, tears in her eyes. "What's the matter with you?" I said. "What's the matter with her?"

"I think this is something you two need to discuss. I'll be in the other room, if you have any questions, Mr. Ivory," he said, walking away.

"You better talk to me, girl. What you done did? Catch something?"

She stayed quiet.

"Answer me," I said, grabbing her by the shoulders.

"I don't want you to be mad."

"Too late for that. I already am. And you gonna see me get a lot more mad if you don't tell me something. What'd he say?"

"You promise not to beat me?"

"Why would I do that? You ain't did nothing wrong."

She looked at me as if she did do something though.

"Well, did ya?"

"I had a miscarriage."

"A what? Girl, who you been fucking? You only been back on the prime for a couple of weeks. So who ya been fucking? I know it wasn't me, because I been away."

"I ain't been fucking nobody."

"You gonna lay right there and lie? You not supposed to be fucking unless I tell you to. So who you think the father was? And it better not be who I'm thinking either, bitch." I folded my arms.

She turned back toward the wall. I grabbed her back over. She pulled back, and I snatched her by the wrist. "Who was it?" I said.

"Gordy."

"What? My brother?" I slapped her in the face. "You slept with my brother?"

"It wasn't nothing planned. It just happened like that, baby."

"Oh, it just happened like that, huh? You just accidentally opened your legs, and he fell in, right? Right?" I said, raising my voice. "You better start saying something quick." I pulled off my belt.

"It just happened, Coke. There ain't nothing else I can say."

"Let's go," I said, pulling her off the bed. "Get on your feet."

"The doctor didn't say I could go yet."

"I don't give a shit what the doctor said. We is going. I'm going to kick your ass when we get home."

The doctor walked from the back room through a curtain. "Excuse me, sir. Mr. Ivory, is there a problem?"

"No problem at all. I'm just taking my wife on home now. She's feeling a lot better. Ain't cha, baby?" I squeezed her wrist.

She sniffled. "I'm fine."

"No. I think you should stay about another half hour. Your body still needs to adjust," he told her, while looking at me.

"Naw. I'm in charge of her. Sign her ass out of here right now."

"Sir, I'm going to have to insist you allow her to stay a while longer."

I snatched Cakes by the arm and pulled her onto the opening elevator.

When we arrived back at home I started sending some of the boys out to find Gordy. I told them not to come back unless they heard something or found him, and not necessarily in that order.

"Get the fuck over here," I yelled at Cakes.

She ignored me and continued strolling up the stairs. The African girls was scurrying throughout the house, getting ready for tonight. They stayed far away from my yelling. They feared me because on my ship I was master. I took my shoe off my foot, and all twelve of them stopped in their tracks.

"Cakes," I yelled. I threw the shoe at the back of her head. Then I ran up the steps behind her and pulled her back down by her ponytail.

She screamed and swung at the air. "No!"

"Shut up," I said, repeatedly slapping her face. "Just shut up."

"Please . . . I'm sorry."

The girls covered their faces and cried.

"Shut the hell up," I told them all. "You wanna be a slut, bitch?" I shook Cakes. "Sleep with my brother . . . "I slapped her to the floor.

She tried crawling away, but I put my foot on her back and stood on it. She let out a long, drawn-out scream. I knelt down and popped her in the head with my knuckles. "You done disrespected me for the last time."

I went to beat her in the head again, and one of the girls yelled out. Before I could turn around, they all jumped on my ass, armed with pots and pans, nails, and heels. Some sank their teeth down into any body part they could reach, while the others took turns beating me to the floor with kitchen utensils.

"Stop, stop, you crazy li'l bitches. Stop," I said, blocking the attack squad's assault with my forearm.

Cakes pushed herself up off the floor and balanced herself against the stove. She reached for a pot of boiling noodles then stood over me with it.

I looked up at her. "You better think about what you doing, girl."

Tears flooded her eyes, and both her hands shook, causing a drop of boiling water to splash on my cheek.

"Ah shit!" I grabbed the side of my face. "Watch what you doing, bitch."

The girls all laughed as I lay helpless under Cake's steaming pot of payback.

"Go, go, go," the girls chanted in their native language.

Cakes slowly began to tip the pot.

"Cakes, don't do it," I said, closing my eyes down hard.

"Go, go, go," they continued.

"Please, Cakes . . . I'm sorry."

"When I said sorry, did you listen to me?"

"Baby, I love you."

"Fuck you, Solomon."

As soon as the words slipped out of her mouth, the downpour of noodles and piping hot water tortured my face and neck. I screamed until my tonsils blocked my esophagus.

"How you like it, punk?" She kicked me in the ribs. "Let's go, y'all," she said to the girls.

They all mimicked Cake's confident bop in her neck and a hand on her hip. As they walked toward the front door, the very last one in line turned back to me, swung her hips, then winked. They all looked back and laughed.

"I'ma get you, Cakes. Won't be nowhere you can hide."

"Whatever," she said, opening the door.

Blam!

Cakes' head split apart, and her body back-flipped across the living room.

The killer held all the girls at bay and ran over to me aiming. "Don't say shit. Just listen." He pulled his ski mask down snug under his chin. "You got less than two seconds to tell me where that bitch-nigga Gordy at."

"I ain't seen him," I said, holding my hands up.

"Wrong answer." He smashed the butt of the shotgun into my shoulder. "Try again," he said, reloading.

"Ay, nigga. Don't even turn around, nigga." Gordy quickly ran over to the man and put his nine right to his temple and pulled the trigger, sending the girls screaming up the stairs.

"We gotta get outta here," I said, reaching up to his hand. "Damn, Cakes!" I jumped over her body.

We hopped into his black Maxima. He put a siren up in the windshield and closed the tinted windows.

"This'll divert they attention for a minute," he said driving frantically down a residential street, both hands gripping the wood-grain steering wheel tight.

I looked at him. "Where you been, Gordy? Why you just up and disappeared like that? Niggaz usually only do shit like that when they done did something wrong. You do something wrong?"

"First of all, nigga, I just saved your life, so act like you thankful. Secondly, we ain't kids, nigga. We is men. Me, I'm a man. I go and come as I damn well please, just like your little girlfriend, Mack."

I grabbed on to the coat rack as we made a sharp right turn. "What's that supposed to mean?"

"I looked up to you, man. You was like my hero. I wanted to be like you."

"Nigga, you could've never been like me. You never could and never will be. You the type nigga who just shoot and don't gain nothing from it. What part of the game is that? How the fuck you gonna make money if you just shooting a nigga and running? Huh? Who was the nigga in my house about to kill me but looking to kill you?"

"Oh. Just somebody I paid to kill Cakes before she start talking to the *D*'s too."

"That's bullshit. He asked for you."

"Fuck it then," he said, finally merging into traffic on the Northern State Parkway. "I paid him to kill you, and her hooker ass was just in the way, is all."

I grabbed onto him, and we swerved in and out of the fast-moving traffic. He pushed the pedal down and accelerated our drift up and down the slopes of the winding parkway. By this time, we'd already exceeded the speed limit, leaving all the other vehicles behind.

"You sent somebody to kill me? Your brother?"

"You not my brother, you're a fag, fucking homo."

I released my grasp. "What the fuck is you talking about?"

A helicopter above shined its giant spotlight through Gordy's moonroof.

"I saw the shit, man, the initiation. You fucked him, that's how he got in. And the worst part of it all is, you taped it. There ain't nothing you can say. You and that bitch is busted. But you won't embarrass me, though," he said, trying to outrun the light.

Far ahead we could both see the flashing police lights beyond the horizon.

"We can't go any further, man. Stop the car before you get us killed."

"I'm not going to jail." He reached in his cup rest for a sniff.

As police cars behind us began to ride the bumper, Gordy pushed it to the max.

I fell back deep in my seat. "Gordy, stop, man, stop," I yelled, looking back as two police cars pulled up on both sides.

As we neared the forthcoming sirens, spikes was laid out to prevent our escape.

"I'm not going to prison." Gordy opened the door and bailed out.

The car swerved right and hit one police car, then smashed through the guardrail, and rolled into the woods. A second later, a huge tree blocked my view.

The last thing I felt was the skin rip off my face when I hit the windshield.

Chapter Fifty-three

Mack

"I got some bad news and some good news, guys," Jeff said.

"Nothing can be worse than this bullshit here."

"Think not? Looks like Cocaine and Gordy went on a little killing spree last night. We've got them both red-handed. Well, not exactly both. Your boy Gordy jumped out his car while doing about one hundred and twenty miles an hour. He rolled off into a barrier and broke his neck. Cocaine's in critical condition right now."

"Okay, and you're telling me all this because?"

"Because, homeboy"—he picked up my fitted cap and placed it backwards on my head—"if you can't give up anything better than what we have right now, then all three of you niggers is going back to the cage."

"You said I'd be on top? After all this, I can do my thang?"

"Yeah, that's right. Pimping ain't easy, boy. Sometimes you gotta pay. So we straight?"

"Yep. Long as Ton and Sade is."

"They're cool. Now me and Bobby is about to ride on out to the hospital to see about your boy. Oh shit. Is he ever going down. There is a god," he said, closing the door behind him as he walked out.

My chances of escape was nothing more than just a mere thought summoned up by the nigga in me. But this was really it. I was officially part of the "go-tell-it-on-the-mountain" committee, a fucking snitch if I'd ever seen one. Snitch or not, though, this shit was about money and who could control the most of it. And now, with Coke out of the way, I could finally shine like the born star I truly was.

Cocaine's condition improved by the end of the week. They posed questions at him from every direction the instant he opened his eyes. The first two people he got to see after waking up from what he thought was all a bad dream was them bitches, Jeff and I-love-sucking-my-partner's-dick Bobby, ready to cuff him before reading him his rights.

Cocaine was finally convicted upon every charge but credit card fraud. I was ashamed of myself for a second and tried to avoid direct eye contact with him inside the courtroom. When our eyes met, I could see a tears shimmering in the corners of his. I'd betrayed him to save my own ass. At the same time this was for my rise to the top.

Sade wasn't able to contribute much, but what she did tell was enough to get her off. And, Ton, well, he just put the nail in the coffin, once he told who gave the order to murder those two cops. The jury didn't even care why. Cocaine had ordered the assassination of two white cops, and that was worth the death penalty on any planet you lived.

When he was handed down his life sentence, he looked over at me and shook his head in dismay. "You stabbed me in the back. I hope you burn in hell. Bitch, you turn on the only muthafucka who ever gave a shit about you?" He shouted, "Fuck you, nigga!"

"Order in my courtroom!" The judge banged his gavel on the sounding block. "Order in the court!"

Cocaine spat at the judge. "Fuck you, honky!"

The judge told the guards, "Get him out of here." And they dragged him out kicking and screaming, and cursing me.

After a while I found it humorous and laughed at him. "Told you this was going to be mines," I said, gloating as the guards used brute force to remove him. I turned toward the back to see Jeff and Bobby smiling and giving me a thumbs-up.

Chapter Fifty-four

Mack

Everything was looking top-notch for a nigga. My wolves was back in effect, and I now had double the amount of girls I had before, including those little African bitches. Jeff and Bob worked their corruptive magic and pulled some bullshit out their hat to make that work.

I got Joi back. Jeff and Bob had been holding her captive until that whole thing had blown over. Sade disappeared, and that was the last anybody saw of her. Ton stayed with me, and I gave him the position he always wanted, my right-hand man. He didn't complain because he finally was getting the paper he wanted. His recognition meter shot up like Jeff's blood pressure. People said his name wherever he walked.

I was back up in the office of Phenomenon taking calls when Joi walked in. "What's good, babe?" I said, my feet up on the desk. I picked up my burning Cuban cigar from my crystal ashtray.

She put her Prada purse on the desk. "You got to do that soon as I walk in?"

"Yo, let me call you back," I said over the phone. "What's up your ass?"

"Nothing good, man. I went to the doctor today."

"And?"

"And I'm three months pregnant," she said casually. My feet dropped off the desk, and I sprung up. "You are? For real? That's what's up." I smiled and walked around the desk to hug her, but she didn't hug me back. "What's the matter?" I said, sitting on the edge of the desk. "You not happy?"

"I wanted to see what you wanted to do, but no matter what you say, I already got my mind made up."

"What you mean, you already got your mind made up?"

"Why are you so happy? I thought you'd be telling me to get rid of it."

"Why would I say that? My first child? Never that."

"Exactly. Never that."

"What's that supposed to mean?"

"It means you could never be a father. Look at you. Look at all of this." She pointed toward the dance floor on the lower level. "What kind of father you think you'd be?"

"Don't you start trying to preach to me, Joi. You was loving this example the night I freed your ass from Stan's house."

"That's the wrong example. Yeah, you came up in there, but I freed myself because your bitch-ass was too scared to shoot him. Yeah, I had to shoot him. You running around here fronting like you was bussing your gun. I let you rock my title because I loved you, but this shit now is just too crazy for me. I don't like this life no more, and I don't want it for my child. That's why after it's born I'll be leaving."

"Leaving? You're not going anywhere with my child."

"What you gonna do? Hold me prisoner like how your boy had Cakes? You're not. Walk away from this right now, and we can bounce. We got the money, baby. You don't got to do this no more."

"What about when the money run out, then what, Joi? Where you going to work at? What skills you got . . . because that's the only way you going to find a job that'll pay you halfway decent?"

"I'm not going to be selling my ass for the rest of my life."

"You ain't had to sell your ass in about two years, so cut out the bullshit."

"Everything with you is always bullshit when it's not going your way."

"You heard what I said, Joi. You not going anywhere. My baby will be just fine. I got the streets on my side, the cops on my side, and plenty of surrogate mothers to help out. The shit's a fucking luxury. You better take advantage."

It was four in the morning when I hooked up with Storm. I'd say we both had a little too much too drink. Phenomenon was closed, but the bar was open. And you know how shit go? One thing led to another, and it can go down like that. The leather mini-skirt she was wearing lifted when I bent her over.

She grabbed the brass sliding pole and gripped it tightly. She begged for me to stroke it hard while she grabbed my dick and pulled it. "Fuck me in my ass, playa," she said, wiggling it at me. She released a loud squeal of pleasure as the head of my saliva-lubricated dick entered her, panting and pulling the back of my left thigh with her right hand.

I slowly eased myself in until my nuts hung directly under the bottom of her apple. She then moved me back some and pulled herself forward just a little before easing back down on it. I began pumping in and out, as her ass began to secrete a flood of lust from her dark cavern, her D-sized titties bouncing up and down and around to her back.

Suddenly, when the music came on, along with the dance floor lights, I jerked back and turned my head.

She grabbed my leg. "Why you stopping, boo?" she said, looking back over her shoulder.

"The music . . . how it come on?"

"Probably a short in the electric. Now you better finish beating this, playa."

"That shit ain't never happen before."

"Boo, all the doors is locked. You locked them yourself. You tripping, and your dick is going down."

My limp dick slid out and popped as it exited. "So do something to get it back up."

She got on her knees and put it right in her mouth, rolling her tongue around my head until "project erection" came to be. She increased the pace of her head nod until I was straight as a reformed criminal. She grabbed the base of it with both hands and looked it straight in the eye. Twisting her head to the side, she wrapped her lips right under the ring of my head and locked them there with a luscious grip of suction.

That went on for the duration of the night, amongst several other positions of fucking.

After that night, she became my number one bitch. I wasn't moving her in with me though. She was like the new and improved version of Cakes, except I kept her in business and didn't try to wifey her up. Y'all get that? I didn't have to beat the bitch-ass because I was jealous. That's what I never understood with Coke—He go and fall in love with a prostitute then turn around and get mad when she's turning tricks. The shit is bogus.

I stayed in business because I didn't have to beat my bitches into submission. Don't get me wrong now. I didn't give no ho respect, but I did show her love because she was part of my extended family. And that love alone right there made any bitch with nothing feel like something. Fuck respect! They needed love. Even if it was under a false impression. I loved them for the money they made me. They loved me for the position I put them in to make that money. That's why you got nine-to-five niggaz running around talking about they love they job. They love the position they been placed in to make that money. Then what they do with it? They come here and spend it on these hoes. It's what I call the circle of synchronicity, the act of following a repetitious method of extra-marital pleasure. Everybody gained. The men got what they want, which was what they were lacking at home from the old ball and chain, and the hoes got an opportunity to become official go-getters. And I just kept getting richer. Is that the American fucking way or what, people?

What you really think be happening to these bitches that turn up missing? Ain't nobody kidnapped nobody. These bitches got out here into college or just fed up with the rules of living at home, the stress of knowing for the rest of their lives they have to provide for themselves. They look at the shit like dudes look at the entertainment business. But just because you break into a luxurious house doesn't mean you'll make it out alive. You won't necessarily be rich. Comfortable. Loved. Or even respected. In this life all you'll ever be remembered for is what you brought to the table. Now, is you gonna be some ol' slave nigga who just bring home the bacon, or the breadwinner who hands out the sandwiches with the bacon in between?

Chapter Fifty-five

Anton

Me and Gordy had never been the best of friends, but we shared the same animosity toward Mack. I'm lying. His shit was a little more extreme. It was good to be home. You'd think that niggaz woulda tried pounding me out after Cocaine went down, but it wasn't like that. We established some new rules. We was only here to ensure that these bitches made the money. No more, no fucking less. Even though things was going fine and I wasn't tripping on Mack no more, the air just wasn't feeling right. I mean, the air around him was thin. His officialness was beginning to lack, and it showed.

"Ton," my moms called as I walked up from the basement.

"What's good, ma?"

"The phone, boy."

"Who is it?" I said, reaching for it from her hand.

"It sound like that detective."

"All right." I took the call into the living room. "Yo."

"Yo, homeboy, it's your main nigger, Ton. Why don't you bounce on out that crib and take a ride with me and my peoples?" Detective Jeffery laughed over the phone.

"Man, what y'all want? I'm mad busy right now."

"It'll only take a second. You mean to tell me that you can't give us a couple seconds of your time . . . after all we did for you?"

"I'm coming out. Two minutes is all y'all got."

I stepped into the back seat of the midnight blue Intrepid, its windows tinted so black, no one could see inside.

"Ay, Anton, how ya doing?" Bobby said.

"I'm chilling, yo, maintaining, know what I'm saying?"

"I love it when you talk like that," Jeff said. "Know what I'm saying?"

"A'ight. When you finish sounding stupid, you can tell me what you need to tell me so I can get the fuck outta here."

"Drive, Bobby." Jeff sipped his coffee. "Shit," he yelled out.

Bobby had sped down the block right into a pothole and Jeff's coffee jumped out his hands and onto his lap.

"Goddamn it, Bob," he said, fanning his crotch, "you trying to kill me. Pull the damn car over, asshole."

We didn't get very far, but I wasn't trying to be seen with these dudes. I slid down under the tinted windows. "Come on, man, y'all can't be having me out here like this."

"Shut the fuck up. I'm just shaking this shit off of my pants."

We quietly rode to Rockaway Beach and parked near the boardwalk. The city lights sparkled from across the ocean's surrounding shorelines. Small boats cruised past each other with the motor on low, the full moon casting her sexy and persuasive body of illumination across the bed of liquid.

We walked to the boardwalk and sat on some wooden benches a couple hundred feet away from the incoming tide. I could smell and taste the misty spray of diluted salt in the air. It made me choke.

"There, there," Jeff said, patting my back.

"I'm a'ight, man," I said, spitting up. "Okay, what the fuck y'all want? I'm a free man, and the shit is documented and on file."

"Our backs are against the wall right now, Anton," Bobby began. "Our backs are against the wall, and we're going to need your help again."

"Aw no. Y'all not getting me caught up in that business again. Naw."

"Let me ask you something, Anton," Bobby said, "Are you happy with your freedom? Because there was a lot of red tape to cut through to make that work. Did you really think that just your snitching kept you out?"

"It's what you said would be to my advantage. I took advantage of the opportunity and seized it. So why am I here? We don't got no more ties. Your business is with Mack."

"How you feeling about that asshole nowadays?" Jeff asked.

"He a'ight. I ain't got no static against him or nothing."

"That's good. How's he paying you?"

"Look, man, I'm gone. You all up in my business like I owe you a favor or something."

"All right, Anton," Jeff said. "I'm going to be up front with you. Something was found inside Gordy's car under the floor mat, something that has to do with nothing, but at the same time, everything."

"Huh?"

"We found Mack's initiation on DVD."

"So?"

"After all this time no one is interested anymore about this guy's credibility?"

"I could give a shit less. He ever come at me wrong, I'm knocking him out. What his initiation got to do with me?"

"You're second in charge, right? What he does reflects on you, and vice versa."

"Yeah, go on. I'm listening."

"Basically, what Jeff is trying to say is Mack has to go. Not just Mack, but the entire operation. I.A.'s been doing a lot of snooping around lately, and we can't afford to let this shit blow up in our faces."

"So again, why the fuck talk to me? You have nothing on me. I been clean since all this shit been over. What incited this new operation anyway?"

"Your boy is stupid. Get in the car. I want you to see something."

We sat inside the car, and Bobby slid a DVD inside the portable player sitting up on the dashboard.

"I'm not fien'ing to watch no movies with y'all."

"Shhh," Bobby said, leaning back in his seat.

I was caught up in a zone of betrayal and disgust by the time it was over. Bobby hit the stop button and turned toward me in the back seat. "So, whadda ya think? Think ol' Mack got the talent to be best supporting actor?"

"He sure looked happy," Jeff commented. "Now what kind of man you want over you that does something like that? This is your reputation at stake. We can get you set up in another city."

"If I snitch though, right?"

"Not this time. What we need for you to do is expose him to his people. The rest will take care of itself."

It wasn't even a question of working with these dudes again. It was about principle. And apparently this dude had none. I was tight because all this time everybody wondering why he got this privileged status. Coke's own brother, God bless the dead, his own brother didn't even had the pull he did. Now I knew why, and soon, so would everyone else. I knew just where to do it at too—The Big Ballerz Bash in Chi-Town next month.

"So, tell me why I'm doing this again. I mean, what's it really all about? And what's in it for me?"

"It's all about economy," Bobby said.

"Economy?"

"Economy," they reiterated simultaneously.

"I'm not understanding."

"Mack's taking the business away from the drug dealers and putting them on with him. That means the street money is not going back into the government. You know what I'm talking about. If we kill him, the public will know it was a conspiracy because they love him so much, like he's some kind of fucking hero or something."

"So? Why use me?"

"Because you're the closest one to him. He trusts you," Bobby said. "He has to go. We didn't anticipate it turning out like this. I was kind of starting to like him. But the bottom line is that he's out of here. Too much of a chance that he could gather all the criminals up and start a war in New York. We can't have that."

"I don't know, man. I don't need this shit on my head again. I ain't tryin'a get the nigga killed."

"You wanted to kill him before," Jeff said. "What, freedom done made you go soft?"

"Ain't nobody gone shit. I don't like dude 'cause he ain't real. But I don't got that much hate for him to get murked."

"Nobody said anything about killing anyone," Bobby said. "We just said he has to go. Soon! I got a couple of more movies for you to take a look at. Gordy was talking to us for a while when his brother was away. He was trying to work out a deal with us to get rid of his brother and Mack. He was giving us information and also these." He pulled two more movies from the glove compartment. "I think you'll want to watch this alone. Get on up in the front seat. I'm going to take a piss. Hey, Jeff, my doctor said I shouldn't carry anything heavy." He laughed and got out the car.

"You should've thought about that before you married that pig."

"She's working on her weight."

"Only thing she's working on is how much butter it'll take to rub around the sides of the tub so she can slide in."

I sat back and pressed play.

"Drink, nigga, drink," Gordy said, laughing.

Mack was getting head and kissing Storm. Gordy continued passing him drinks while the strippers rubbed they titties in his face. After the show was over, whoever was taping the party followed the girls into the dressing room.

Gordy walked ahead of the camera and turned around. "Welcome to the exposure room." He laughed. "Hey, bitches, that nigga Gordo in the building. That was a good job y'all did tonight. Where muthafucking Storm's ol' freaky ass at?"

The cameraman walked across the room, zooming in on all the various-shaped tits and trimmed bushes. Some girls covered up; others shook them and pinched their nipples. Some even kissed the lens of the camera. He stopped at a door, and Gordy pounded on it.

"Open up, ya big sexy. Open the fucking door." Gordy laughed in his drunken state.

The door slowly opened, and the camera aimed at the black leather heels she was wearing. It slowly crept up her body to her large chest, and finally her face. She was wiping the remainder of thick earth-tone makeup to conceal her obvious masculine features. Gordy had gotten this nigga drunk and had him chilling with a transvestite. Everybody was in on it. And now so was I.

"Storm!" I pounded on her apartment door. "Storm!" I pounded again, not waiting on a response.

"This better be good," she said from behind the door. "Who is it? It's three o'clock in the morning."

The door opened, and I looked her straight in the eyes. "Can I come in?"

"I don't know, Ton. It's kind of late, and I have to get an early start in the morning, you know how it is."

"This'll only take a minute. I just need to ask you a few questions."

"Well, okay. Long as it don't take all night. You want to sit down?"

"Naw, I don't want to sit down nowhere in here. I'm gonna get right to the point. You a man," I said, pulling out my gun.

She nervously said in her seductive voice. "Baby, are you crazy?"

"I saw the dressing room digital after you and Mack did the thing. You a dude. Why'd Gordy pay you to do that?"

He began in that fag voice, "I—"

I lifted my gun before he could go on. "Speak regular." I warned.

"Oh God, please don't kill me," he whimpered as his hands shook. "He wanted to prove to everybody that Mack was a fag. He wanted everybody to stop loving him so much. So he paid me to do what I do, then make it look like he knew about it all along. That would shut his whole shit down."

"So you mean to tell me that he still don't know? That's bullshit. He knew. How the fuck you don't know how a man look?"

"I fooled you. The men in the club. I don't let them feel in between my legs. And even if they do accidentally come across it they usually never question it. That's why they drink until they're drunk. They figure there ain't no accountability for their actions if under the influence."

"Is that so?"

"Oh God, I think I just tinkled myself," he said, covering up his crotch area.

"You don't try disappearing nowhere. You is going to tell everybody about this at the ball next week. We're going to expose this together. Then you gonna leave New York. Got a problem with that?"

"It's all about you, boo."

"Don't be calling me that shit. Fucking homo!" I said, slamming the door behind me as I walked out.

Chapter Fifty-six

Mack

Not that it really mattered to me that Glen was my father, but I still felt compelled to go and see him. I wanted to give him a piece of my mind. I wanted him to see that without his presence in my life I'd still become successful.

"You got no reason to be here," he heartlessly said.

"I got every reason to be here. I just wanted to see the bitch who deserted his son. That's all I'm here to do. I ain't trying to bond with no nigga in my manhood, father or no father."

"Oh really? Nothing like when you was looking up to my cousin, huh?"

"That was different. He gave me more fatherhood than you ever could. Look at you. Even now you in denial. I'm glad they got your deadbeat ass up in here. You always get caught sooner or later. Do you even remember who my moms was?"

"She was a crackhead, boy. A stone-cold chimney-stacksmoking whore. Way before you was even around. And that's the God's honest truth. I say that to say if I'd known your momma was pregnant I would've did the right thing."

"The right thing? Is that why you got a second child running around somewhere in the world that you ain't never met?"

"Boy, where you think you get it from? Fucking bitches run in the family. But I done heard some next shit about you. And you doing more than just fucking bitches. I know all about you and Solomon's little secret. Don't know how it stayed a secret for so long, but when the truth comes out you'll be one sorry bastard."

"Why'd you think trying to connect me and Joi to the killing you did would work? Once those blood samples come back you're fucked."

"I'm fucked? Your whole career is built on bullshit, Mack. Those detectives are dirty as a muthafucka and you fuck with them, just like Solomon did. Look where he at now. You get used to this setting, boy, because it may not be today, and it may not be tomorrow. But your ass is going down. And for your sake, you better pray it's in prison and not the ground."

"Oh, so now you wanna step up and give advice? Well, fuck you, nigga. I just came here to

see the bitch who abandoned his responsibilities.
Look at me. I became something without you to
teach me nothing."

"What you done did that you think I'm supposed to be impressed or shocked?"

"I became successful."

"You became a pimp, and from what I hear,
not a very good one at that."

"There ain't nothing you can say to get under
my skin, old man. Just look where you at then
take a look where I'm at. So fuck you and your
life sentence."

"I'm still your father, and you're not gonna
disrespect me."

I exploded in laughter. "So long, Glen. Happy
life sentence," I said, turning my back on him.

As I walked out the gates of the prison and
looked up at the fourth floor window. "I'm successful," I yelled up toward the window, a pro-
nounced smile of achievement on my face.

Chapter Fifty-seven

Cocaine

"I don't give a shit how you do it. Just get the shit done, nigga. I don't give a fuck about no monitored calls. Fuck them. I'm locked up in here for the next six lifetimes. You think I'm concerned with who's listening? Put that word out that anybody in the way becomes part of the circumstance." I slammed down the phone inside Character Builder prison in upstate New York.

I walked into the rec room and sat in an orange plastic chair. I extended my legs and leaned back. Terror squad members leaned against the hard, cold walls and just stared at me. Something was up because nobody was saying shit. I just started seeing COs conveniently deserting their posts for safety and solitude on the other side of the bars. A big dude walked into the rec room accompanied by a group of lifers. Young lifers. They had nothing to lose and everything to gain. Hop on me and you got yourself a sweet reputation. With nobody from my clique to back me, I just sat motionless.

The dude had to be about twenty-seven or some shit like that. His hair was all wild and bushy. He didn't have a five o'clock shadow growing on his face. He just had a shadow. He stood six-feet six and looked like he wasn't ready for the small talk.

Everyone crowded around as I coolly sat with my arms folded.

"Hey, you Cocaine, right?"

"Yeah. You might've heard of me. Head of OPT. Running that pussy throughout Queens. Hit man one time or another."

"Nigga, did I ask for your resume? Just shut the fuck up and listen. Me and my dudes right here want in on what you got cracking back out in the world. It's not up for debate."

"Well, boy, you must've thought you was talking to some punk muthafucka. Your size don't intimidate me." I raised up.

His first short right cross to my chin unhinged my jaw and shook my brain around inside my skull. An uppercut stood me back up straight off my feet. I fell back into the row of bolted-down plastic seats, then on my face.

The violent uproar of the inmates inspired the corrupt COs to place bets on the winner. Big boy came down with a pounding right but missed when I turned my head. His hand smashed into the hard concrete floor.

I quickly scrambled to my old-ass feet and kicked him in the ribs. He grabbed my leg as he stood and lifted me above his head.

"Throw him, throw him," the inmates chanted.

I waved my arms in the air as he prepared to propel me across the room. Which is just what he did. I slammed, back first, into the steel bars and dropped. As he went to take a running jump onto my head, the midnight hopper was halted in his tracks by rubber bullets. The bullets sunk deeply into his flabby mold and dropped him like dimes. We both were immediately pulled to our feet and jerked around.

The inmates, still amped off the melee, began arguing, but that was taken care of quickly, and we were each sent to the hole for one month.

The instant I came out the hole the warden wanted to see me.

"How are you feeling, Mr. Ivory?"

"How you think I'm feeling, man? I'm fresh out the hole."

"All right, you just be easy. You'll be back to your cell after I ask you some questions."

"Yeah."

"What was the fight about last month?"

"What fight?"

"The altercation between you and Duane Faison."

"Huh?"

"D-Gunz."

"Look, man, why you bothering me about this past shit?"

"I need to know if this is going to cause some kind of friction between your people and his."

"I don't got no people here. Y'all made sure of that before I came. So what retaliation you talking?"

"I mean, in the streets."

"Man, that shit don't even got nothing to do with you. You only the police in here. And before you ask, no, I don't want to press charges for assault. So fuck you and this system."

"You just earned yourself another month in the hole," he said. "Guards, take him back. We'll see you in a month, Mr. Ivory."

Chapter Fifty-eight

Mack

I know earlier I said shit was going smoothly. And it was. Right up until those blood samples from Sade's moms murder scene came back. Naturally, shit came back negative, far as me and Joi was both concerned. Just as before. But this time when they ran Joi's blood across Glen's it was a perfect DNA match. Hence, the missing child he never knew he had. We didn't believe it at first until we did some test. It was right on point. Me and Joi was brother and sister with a child on the way. Joi fainted right inside the doctor's office, his black leather lazy chair catching her fall. Her eye slowly opened with shock and tears in them.

"This goes outside the professional boundaries of my position, but I think that you two are sick. Do you know what's going to happen when the baby is born?" the doctor said.

Nothing was said as Joi and I began to psycho-logically and emotionally detach instantly. We was ashamed and embarrassed. Embarrassed because we both knew what this had to look like. Two sick individuals breaking the core of mo-rality. Ashamed because . . . who the fuck does this happen to? Was that something God could forgive if you didn't know? Or was it just sinful enough sleeping together in the first place?

"This is my punishment," Joi cried, balling up in the chair.

I wanted to reach out to touch her, but our auras repelled one another's.

"There are more tests that can be run if you'd like."

"More tests for what? She's not keeping it. I ain't tryin'a be no father to no retard. Uh-uh, no way."

"That's what should've been said to prevent all of this. I mean, I am really disgusted. And I'm sorry for speaking my mind. But how in the hell do you sleep with your own sister?" He looked at Joi. "Your own brother?"

"See, man, you got it all wrong. We just met for the first time a couple of years ago. I just recently found my father, and she's just finding out today we both got the same father. We didn't know shit until just now. It's creeping me out." I turned away from Joi.

"That's a real weird story."

"But it's true."

I looked over to Joi as she sat curled up in a fetal position, her thumb in her mouth. She was in a catatonic state, and the doctor said it'd be best if she stayed at the hospital overnight.

"No, I wanna go home," she protested, immediately snapping out of her hypnotic trance.

"We can't hold her if she doesn't want to stay," he said, still looking on in disgust, as if everything I just told him was bullshit.

Truth be told, I wouldn't believe that shit neither. You know why? Because look at what type shit the crackers be doing—fucking they pets, devirginizing their own daughters before puberty, eating their kids in some satanic sacrifice. And he gonna look at me funny?

When we got home Joi went straight upstairs. I called Ton and told him I wouldn't be at the club tonight, so he'd have to hold it down for dolo. I flopped back on the couch and tossed my feet up on the coffee table. My cell rang just as I began to doze off.

"Yeah?"

"Hey, boo. It's Storm. Whatcha doing tonight?"

"I'm dealing with some issues right now. I'ma have to holla at you later."

"Oh, I just wanted to see you for a minute."

"I said no." I turned the power off on my cell and clicked on the stereo.

I've been so many places in my life and time

I always liked this song. It felt like he was telling me about my life. The people watching. The constant acting. The never ending show.

A constant crashing from upstairs interrupted the flow. I ran up the stairs and opened the door. Joi had wrecked the room and was standing on the other side of the bed naked.

"Why is you looking at me?" she said, taking swipes at me from across the room. "Stop looking, you dirty muthafucka."

"Joi, what you doing with that glass?" I said. "Give it here." I attempted to reach for it.

"Stay back." She swung. "I'm not having this baby. He's gonna be born a sin-baby. And it's all our faults."

"Come on, Joi, we can talk about it like brother and sister." I reached out again.

She poked herself twice in the stomach, enough to get a nice flow of blood going. "You think I'm playing?" she yelled. "Stay back. Why it had to be like this, Mack? Why we had to grow up fucked up then get this too? I don't wanna live with this on my head."

"Joi, you talking crazy. Just drop the glass and get some sleep. You be better by the morning."

"It's just always that simple with you. You just sleep everything off. I can't do that, not with this. I am your fucking sister and we're having a baby. I hate you." She spat at me. "I'm taking him with me," she said, wiping blood off her stomach.

"What?" I quickly leaped over the bed to grab her.

She took one step back and slit her right wrist clean through, and blood gushed to the ceiling from the deep incision, spraying graffiti on the paneled walls. She dropped to the floor and began convulsing.

"Joi," I yelled frantically. I wrapped a pillow-case around the wound and quickly dialed nine-one-one, but she died before I could hang up the phone.

"Oh no! Joi." I lifted her by the back of her head into my embrace. "No," I cried, squeezing her tighter.

When the ambulance and police arrived in front of the house, I ran down the stairs and let them in.

As she lay there with her eyes opened and her lips tightly shut, they greeted me with, "There's nothing we can do for her." Her bodily function began to give way, and that's when I knew it was final. But all the shit and piss smell in the world wasn't going to let me leave her side until the day she was buried.

Even though my child and sister was gone, it was back to business. They even rescheduled the Ballerz thing, just on the strength of my suffering. But I made it up to everybody.

Chapter Fifty-nine

Mack

"Ton, we got a serious problem," I said to him as he drove to a custom tailor shop in Harlem.

"What's that, doggy?"

"I don't know what Coke was thinking when he got those bitches."

"What's the deal, man?"

"I had them taken out today for a physical."

"And?"

"And all them bitches is HIV-positive. The hood is infected."

"The hood been infected. I tell you what, though . . . a lot of niggaz is gonna be wondering where they got the shit. Where you think they gonna look first? Who you think they gonna be looking at? They can't look at Coke. He gone. They gonna be looking at Mack. I don't know how you gonna fix this. Every last one of them?"

"Every nappy-headed Negro in the bunch. Fucking Coke, he got jerked. Now what the fuck am I supposed to do with them?"

"Take 'em back from whence they came. Coke keep everything on file. We gather them up and take 'em back tonight."

Later that night we did just that. No phone call or e-mail. We just hopped in three separate Vs and a van that one of my menz used when he was out painting. We stuck the bitches in back of it then rolled on out into the Hamptons.

Me and Ton walked to the door. I knocked.

A voice from behind the door said, "What's your business here?"

"I'm here to return some shit that belong to you."

"Like what?"

"Some li'l slaves."

A series of locks clicked, and the door opened. A man in a white suit stood inside of the screen door. "Gentlemen," he said, clicking on the porch light, "you have something to return? I don't think we've ever done business together."

"Technically we have. You sold something to Cocaine that I inherited. The shit is contaminated. You knew that when you sold them."

"I don't need any problems. You can leave them, but there'll be no refund."

"Fuck it. Just take 'em."

Ton opened the back doors to the van, and they all jumped out then huddled around each other. They shivered in the overly cool night's unpredictable weather.

"Let me ask you something."

"Shoot."

"What are you going to do with them now?"

"In Europe there's an underground slavery ring that only will buy young black girls. They use them to clean the house. Mind their rug rats. Maintain the garden. It's a growing trend. I can't wait for it to catch on." He laughed and walked away, and the girls happily followed behind him into the nearby horse stable.

Chapter Sixty

Anton

I flew out to Chi-Town a day earlier than Mack to set things up. We rented a hall downtown, and I was making sure all the food we ordered was being prepared. Checked on the liquor stockade, the sound system, the lights, the fire exits.

"Yeah, everything looking copasetic," I said to Mack over the phone. "This is going to be big, dude. Yeah, I'll be there to pick you up from the airport tomorrow. Holla," I said, hanging up.

I locked up then closed the doors to the hall. A silver Continental with tinted windows waited for me in the parking lot. I stepped inside and poured a shot of vodka.

"Where to, sir?" the driver asked.

"The Lakefront Hotel. I'm not in a rush, so take the scenic route."

"Yes, sir." From I-90/94, we exited Ohio Street and proceeded two blocks. We turned left on Illinois and went ten more blocks until we crossed Columbus Drive. And the hotel sat lovely as it wanted to, smack dab at the intersection between Illinois and Columbus. It was busy out there. Rolling suitcases was pulled up and down the parking lot. Valet drivers respectfully rejected tips, only to get double that amount for being humble.

"Milton, my dude, good looking." I handed him a twenty. I walked inside the spacious lobby and looked up at the tall trees growing up from under the hotel's surface. Birds flew back and forth above the branches, their shadows casting down each time they flew past the open sky light. I walked forward toward the long gray marble registration desk that sat about twenty feet across and five feet high.

"Hi." The Marsha-Brady-looking bimbo smiled with her fucking disgusting-ass retainer.

"Hey, I'm supposed to be picking up a key. Anton."

She ran her finger down two pages worth of entries before finally stopping. "What room is that, sir?"

"Uh, seventy-five B, I think. Yeah, matter of fact, that is it."

"Cash or credit?"

"Oh, just look in your computer. It's already covered."

"I see. Okay then. All I need is some identification, and you're on your way."

After the song-and-dance routine, I followed the blue trail of carpet leading to the glass elevator. It softly hummed as its double doors smoothly slid open. I quickly closed them, so I could enjoy the ride by myself, especially since I wanted to puff my clip. I inhaled the shit, and my eyes widened.

The elevator rose over the city and showcased the evening skyline's magnificent array of fuchsia, orange, purple, and black. A blimp lazily hovered across the black backdrop promoting Kellz upcoming concert in red dotted lights. Clouds competed to be on the same level as me, but the elevation of my glass shuttle left them coughing up dust. This was as close as you could get to God. *This must be what it feel like to be rising in the wide open after you die.*

The seventy-fifth floor had finally come up. I stepped off the vehicle and made a right down to the end of the hallway. I looked down at the digital key then up at the door. "This is it." I smiled and slid my key inside the groove of the stainless steel lock.

Beep! The door automatically opened, and I walked in. A humongous king-sized bed sat near the balcony window. A large plate window with full-length curtains was in the living room. Reddish-brown carpet with designs on it covered the floor. Large mirrors in the bathroom were clean as looking through a window. The kitchen was equipped with an oven, microwave, and dishwasher. This was it. Five-star suite. *El Presidente.*

I fell back on the bed and bounced off the soft mattress. "Oh, this is what's up," I said, sinking into it.

A knock in the bathroom made me spring up. I crept over to the door with my gun in my right hand. I slowly pushed the door open and quickly felt around for a light switch. It flicked on by itself, and there stood Sade soaking wet from the shower.

"Girl, you almost got yourself shot," I said, putting it back on safety.

"You're late." She walked up to me. "You was supposed to be here hours ago."

"Yeah, I had some li'l shit to take care of. It's all good now."

"Now you promise he not going to get hurt, right?" she asked, her arms sprawled around the back of my neck as I said carried her over to the bed.

"Just his image and pride."

After all the time me and Sade had been spending together, this shit was bound to happen. We hooked up, and nobody ever knew. But they would soon.

Chapter Sixty-one

Mack

"Ladies and gentlemen, this here's another one for the steppas. Deejay Wayne Williams, put the record on. Tell me, what do we do when the deejay's playing our favorite tune?"

It was my night, and I was the sole purpose of this whole gathering. All my wolves was here. Every pimp who had a name came out to pay homage and just have a good time. It was a white-linen affair, and everybody was looking clean. Happy feet slid across the floor and spun around. High heels and shoes screeched the floor and tapped to the rhythm of the music.

Everybody lined up side to side. Men faced the women giving up three feet of personal space. Drinks was tossed up in the air and toasted as those rhythmically imposed steppas dipped down and spun back up, pointing at any bitch that smiled.

I was feeling the love and got all overwhelmed and shit. I was taken aback. I walked into the bathroom and checked under the row of blue stalls. The urinals was also blue and drained fresh water every five seconds. I bent down over the sink and rinsed my face and looked up into the mirror at my reflection. "They love you, boy," I said to myself. "They really love you." I pointed to myself.

Ton walked in. "Hey, you a'ight, man?"

"Yeah," I said wiping my face, "I'm good."

"Your peoples is outside ready to celebrate, nigga. You suppose to be out there."

"Yeah, I'm coming."

"Hey, duke, talk to me. Everything all right," he said, holding me by the shoulders.

"I'm just tripping. All these muthafuckas here for me."

"That's right, you, dude. We here for you." He hugged me. "Yo, I love you, man. You number one in my heart."

"That's what's up," I said, hugging him back.

"Now let's get on out here, ya big pimp!" He laughed and pushed me out the door.

Just then the music stopped, and the spotlight shined on me. I walked through the "soul train" line the crowd had formed. They patted my back and poured champagne on me as I walked by.

Standing on stage was Anton holding a microphone. A movie screen from behind him lowered from the ceiling. "Get on up here, nigga," he said, egging the crowd on to cheer.

I sat on the king throne and was given a pimp cup and some shades.

"Yeah, that's that nigga," Ton said. "Before I get started, let me see if the nigga of the night got some words to say." He laughed and passed me the mike. "Get your ass on up."

"Yo, I just wanna say that it's a real honor to be chilling amongst fellow pimps." I chuckled, but nobody else did. "Ahem, is this thing on?"

"Nigga, sit your ass down." Ton shoved me in the chair.

They all laughed and rooted.

"Now we about to celebrate my man's life. Most muthafuckas start off by telling a nigga's childhood, how he came to be and shit. Well, we ain't gonna start off like that. Can I get an amen?"

"Amen," I said along with the crowd.

"We ain't gonna talk about what school he went to 'cuz we really don't give a fuck where he went to school. Do we? Hell no! Can I get an amen?"

"Amen," we all said.

"See, tonight we gonna just show this man's life for what it really is. The man of many hats fits any head. This nigga know a lot about that. Miko," he holla'd to his man, "run that movie. Congratulations, nigga," Ton said and walked off the stage.

My initiation DVD. I pissed my pants as everyone began looking at each other. The movie showed me and Cocaine going at it. It was his price for my protection. I was scared to death when I went up north. Niggaz was fucking with me, and I didn't know what else to do. That's why I was his number one. Even over Cakes.

The crowd rushing toward me looked like the dirty, black waves of a tsunami.

"Hold up, hold up," Ton said running out on to the stage with his gun aimed. His menz ran out on the stage after him and also held the crowd down. "Now settle down, y'all. Everybody gonna get they turn. You scared, bitch," he said, mushing me. "We ain't done yet, y'all. Roll that next movie."

It was me and Storm fucking on the dance floor a while back. This had to at least prove that I liked women. That is until this video of Storm undressing in the back room, with a dick swinging and everything. I didn't even feel all that. You ever wish you was somewhere other than where you was at?

"Don't make me shoot one of you muthafuck-as," Ton said as the men became more agitated. "Yeah, looks like your night's about to be over. I got one more surprise for you. Come on out, baby."

Sade coolly walked across the stage and into Ton's embrace. Then he walked her over to me and kissed her. "Show 'em the ring," he said.

She extended her hand and flashed her diamond. "You lose this time, Eric," Sade said, walking away.

Ton winked at me. "How ya feel now, pimp?"